Additional Books by Tony Seton

Say It Write

Say It Write

by Tony Seton

June 2021

Carmel, California

Except for *The Young Man and the Sea*, the writings in this book are original works of fiction by Tony Seton. As is the case with most fiction, there have been people, events, and circumstances in the writer's life that have influenced what appears in the pages of his book.

Say It Write

ISBN-13: 978-1-7349057-3-1

Printed in the United States of America

Table of Contents

Author's Note

Back twenty years or so ago, I started producing a weekdaily essay called *SetonnoteS* – yes, a palindrome – that I recorded audio-wise and also posted as a printed version on my eponymous website. The pieces ran about 335 words with a brief open and close, and the two-minute audio version had Liz Story's *Hymn* behind it. I probably produced over 2,000 *SetonnoteS* that were distributed to a whole bunch of radio stations, websites, and print outlets.

Most of the essays were on a single subject, usually current. But sometimes there were a number of things I wanted to report that weren't worth a whole two minutes. So I would produce a *Bits & Pieces* report that might include four or five short elements.

That's something of the explanation for this book, *Say It Write*, which follows the similarly formatted *Selected Writings*, which was published several years ago. In the following pages are twenty pieces of prose, poetry, stage scripts, a letter to the editor, and segments from four books that, though not book length in their own write (sic) were still worth the paper they are printed on.

So you're not going to get stuck starting a full-length book and thinking you have to stay with it or jump out of the boat. That often produces either a sense of guilt for not cleaning the plate, or resentment toward the author for having the brass to write something so, um, unappetizing that he should never have picked up the proverbial quill. With all of these relatively short pieces, you can easily weigh anchor and sail on to the next bite.

And finally there is this non sequitur...I have two fortune cookie fortunes taped to the bottom of my computer screen. They're in front of me all the time, and occasionally I remember to read them. One is from a very long time ago, and it comes up in conversation in the story *Open to Life*. Enjoy it in context.

The other appeared three months ago, on February 29th (of all dates) this year (2020). I had taken my friend and colleague Michelle to lunch at the Full Moon in Monterey. At the end of the meal, the waiter put two fortune cookies in front of me, and I pushed one across the table to Michelle. She shook her head and, pushing it back without opening it, said, "No. That's yours."

Writing this, I didn't remember but at the time, Michelle told me why it was mine. When she was proof-reading this book, she reprised the reason. Aha! There are rules about fortune cookies, and from *The rules of Fortune Cookies* on the *World of Cookies* site, the first two spoke to our situation:

The first is *Do not grab the cookie closest to you, but the one furthest away when served by the host or hostess.* Interesting; maybe from the school of the closest glass has the poison in it. And the second rule is, *Pick a cookie that is most closely "pointing" towards you* (by which they mean the two pointed ends are facing you rather than the rounded part).

Got it? Okay, this is what *my* fortune said:

> *Your individuality provides a light for others.*

That quite bowled me over. I was reminded, again, that synchronicity is a critical factor in my life. And frequently in my writing. In that vein, I touch on the concept of luck and order in the universe in the segment from my book *Deki-san* later in these pages.

Tony Seton
Carmel, California

Sherlock Holmes in Carmel

This was a talk I delivered before the Diogenes Club of Carmel-by-the-Sea in May 2016. In something of a reflection of the polarization of the times – then and now – two of the 25 Sherlockians present expressed their ungracious annoyance at the political nature of my essay. The rest appreciated how the story was told, and particularly the first-person voice of Dr. John Watson, Holmes' official chronicler.

My friend Sherlock Holmes had long spoken of his respect for Alexis de Tocqueville and his esteemed work, **Democracy in America**. The young French nobleman had traveled through the young nation and had recorded a number of significant observations about its unique people. De Tocqueville and a friend had ostensibly been sent by their government to study the American prison system, and while they produced a report on that subject, they used their nine-month trip for their own purpose...a close-up look at the American society.

"Their two most important observations," Holmes declared one cold late winter morning as he sat before the fire pushing a plug of Jamaican Red into a favorite pipe, "were, one, that there was no formal class system in America. Every man could shake the hand of every other man, though of course not everyone did. It was a metaphor."

"And the other?" I prompted him after he seemed lost in thought after his first long, deep toke.

For a moment he looked at me, trying to connect my question to a previous synapse. He quickly made the connection. "And the other was that the American people, according to the French men's experience, were by their nature, less inclined to raise themselves and more to pull their betters down."

I harrumphed as I was wont to do. "Yes, I remember you saying that Holmes." I smiled inwardly as I recognized the detective in me. "And what, pray tell, was it that brought this subject to the fore?"

He flashed his familiar half-second smile acknowledgment at me and replied, "I've been thinking of taking a trip to America, Watson, to see if what they saw then isn't what is defining the not-so-young country still."

"Really, Holmes. You're not intending a visit to the Valley of Fear?"

"Oh, Watson, please," he scoffed bemusedly. "No, and never would I. I have in mind a trip to the far coast. They call it the West Coast, because it is on the west side of their country. Some call it the Left Coast, as many in the three states that border the Pacific Ocean, are of the more liberal persuasion.

I scrunched up my face as I considered his math. "Uh, Holmes, I would remind you that there are five of the American states which border the Pacific Ocean."

"Pshaw," he retorted though amiably. "Of course I know that, Watson, but I have never accepted the wisdom of making Alaska and Hawaii states. They aren't attached to the so-called Lower Forty-Eight. And they were acquired after the Second World War in an embarrassing example of annexation. I place them in the 'other' category."

I harrumphed again and said *sotto voce*, "I see," but that didn't mean that I agreed with him.

He let out a cloud of smoke and most of it was pulled up the flue by the heat of the fireplace, although some of its aroma reached me. Holmes caught me sniffing and extended his Persian slipper to me. "Do have some, my good friend. It would be good for the aches and pains you suffer due to the Jezail bullet you received in the Battle of Maiwand that they were not able to remove from your shoulder."

"Most kind of you, Holmes," I said, removing a pinch of the weed and rolling it in a cigarette paper. Shortly I had drawn two healthy tokes from the joint, and the rest of the day became a blur. The conversation would be picked up the next morning.

* * * * *

"I've made reservations for us to travel to Carmel-by-the-Sea, Watson. I'm trusting that you will join me. We leave on April Fool's Day."

"You're not joking, are you, Holmes?" It was a weak attempt at jocularity.

He responded with a patronizingly benign Mona Lisa-like smile.

"We will fly to San Francisco and then Monterey where we will rent a car to provide local transportation."

"Why this Carmel-by-the-Sea?"

"It is a charming place, I'm told by people whose discernment I hold in high regard. *Quaint* is the most common term used to describe the village. Lots of trees, artists, and people whose idea of progress is turning the clock back to the middle of the last century."

"Why ever would they want to do that, Holmes?"

"That's not clear exactly. Speculation has it that they would like a quieter time, oh yes, and fewer tourists."

"Tourists?"

"Yes, visitors who spend money."

"I knew that, Holmes, but what is their problem?"

"It seems that the tourist industry is what pays to keep

Carmel-by-the-Sea financially afloat, and the locals resent having to deal with the traffic, the crowded restaurants, and particularly their poor taste in comportment."

"Do they have no other sources of revenue?"

Holmes shook his head dismissively. "No, they produce nothing."

"Is it a religious issue that they are unproductive?"

"Possibly something like that. A fiscally lethal marriage of elitist *nimby* and foolishness."

"Nimby?"

"A socio-political acronym for not in my backyard."

"I see," I said, though I didn't really, while at the same time understanding that I didn't have to. The conversation had been sidetracked and needed to be rescued. "What is it you are expecting to discover in this Carmel-by-the-Sea?"

"They are having an election on April 12th, for mayor and for two seats on their city council." He left it there thinking I would insist on elucidation.

I complied. "And?"

"Exactly, Watson, why should it matter that this one-mile-square town of 2500 voters cast its ballots? That is what I mean to find out."

"In April? I thought Americans voted in November, around Guy Fawkes Day?"

"You are ever so prescient, my good fellow, and in this case also correct." He sighed. "It's one of the quaint notions of the people of this town who, despite their eccentricities – and I'm using a polite term here – like to be different just to be different. The purported reasoning is that if their election were held in November, their candidates might be lost on the ballot."

"Bosh!" I huffed.

"You are right to huff, Watson, for the explanation is without foundation. However, as bright as are these people normally, they have a tendency to come off the rails at times. As in this situation, where they cost themselves an extra 20,000 American dollars to show themselves as different."

"That's seems rather extravagant. Couldn't they just put up a banner of some sort?"

"Logic tends to escape their decision-making. Alas, they prefer *ye olde* to common sense."

"Hmm," I said mullingly. "How long are we to spend in this Carmel?"

"Carmel-by-the-Sea, Watson. There is a Carmel in Indiana which is as far away geographically – and as culturally – as you could possibly imagine, and they can be sensitive about it."

"Very well, and...?"

"About two weeks, although to prevent feeling stifled, I anticipate visiting San Francisco for a couple of days mid-stay. To clear out our senses, if you will."

"It sounds like we will need it."

*   *   *   *   *

Our flight was long but thankfully uneventful. Holmes had enjoyed some Maui-Wowie on the drive to the airport and so easily relaxed for the much of the trip. He had asked if I would do the driving while we were in The States, and I said I should be glad to. Indeed, I took a brief driving course in a small town outside London where people drove on the right side of the road so that I might get used to the peculiar American ways. It wasn't as much of a challenge as I thought I might face.

We hired our motor car at the Monterey Regional Airport, and it wasn't but fifteen minutes that we were pulling up in front of the Cypress Inn in Carmel-by-the-Sea. I was most impressed by our lodgings. Our suite was a model of understated elegance and full functionality. After unpacking, we made our way back to the living room of this reconfigured mansion to plan our first foray into our new surroundings, and there we were greeted by a remarkably dapper fellow who turned out to be the co-owner of the inn.

"Welcome to you," said the fellow who introduced himself as one Denny LeVett. "What a pleasure to have such distinguished guests staying with us. Please let me know what I can do to make your stay most comfortable."

"Mr. LeVett," began Holmes, "how very kind of you. We are delighted to be residing in your wonderful establishment."

"Let me add that Doris Day, my partner, asked me to extend her best wishes to you gentlemen. She is a big fan of your work."

"As we are of hers," I piped in

"Regrettably," LeVett explained, "she is involved with a major flamingo rescue fundraiser in Hialeah, Florida, and doesn't expect to return here until the end of the month."

"Alas," said Holmes appropriately mournfully, "She would be a reason alone for us to return. Please pass on to her our felicitations for her fundraiser. If we had a front yard, we would surely get a flamingo for it."

With that we parted, and map in hand, we walked the streets of Carmel-by-the-Sea. It was indeed a charming town, though I think Holmes shared my view that it seemed a little too quaint. As he commented later, "It's one thing to love trees, but it's another to have them block sidewalks and roads. These people can't all be Druids, after all."

Mostly, it seemed, Holmes was making note of the campaign signs in the windows of many of the retail establishments. Of course he'd done his homework before we'd left, and he knew the players, along with their positions on issues, how they presented them-selves, and who were their supporters. The purpose of this first walk through the village, he explained this way: "It is necessary, Watson, to get a feel for the bones of a place. You know that to be the case with a building you might be considering for your office or a home. It is also what you need to sense an election."

"Boots on the ground," I offered, and then added, "so to speak."

"What a deplorable expression, Watson. Boots on the ground speaks of bellicosity and violence. The truth is not boots on the ground but grievously-attacked bodies in the ground." He sniffed, "But of course I take your point. And yes. You know this election year has seen a near total failure of the media – we once called them the press – to properly inform the people about the candidates and the issues, and about what the nation truly needs. At the core of their incompetence was the pressure to report and publish incessantly, and they were often, it seems, too busy talking or writing to explore the matters to any depth. Or even to give time to serious thought."

"I fear the collapse of the Fourth Estate threatens the very sustainability of democracy, Holmes."

"You are so right, Watson."

We ended our long day with an early dinner at Little Napoli, around the corner from the Inn. There we had the good fortune to meet the voluble owner of the restaurant, Rich Pèpe. I say good fortune because the restaurateur was well-informed about the local political situation, and he was free with both facts and opinions on who was running and whether they deserved his support. As I said, Holmes was fully versed on the race and its components, but he welcomed the conversation with Pèpe, a former candidate for mayor himself.

As we walked off our delicious dinner, extending our perambulation back to our lodgings, Holmes reviewed the situation for me. There were five candidates for two city council seats, and two of them – a member of Planning Commission and a hotelier actively involved in many volunteer activities – were by far and away the best qualified. In the mayor's race, the difference between the two candidates was stark. One had served on the council and Planning Commission for more than a decade. He also had an MBA and extensive experience in private sector business. And he had been endorsed by every political leader and former mayor. The other man had been brought up locally, hadn't finished college, and had only worked for his mother to maintain the many properties she owned.

"The key to the mayor's race is that the qualified candidate has been tied to the current mayor who made some mistakes. His challenger is playing up those mistakes well out of proportion; in fact he has lied about the retiring mayor and his alleged misdeeds, falsely tarring the serious candidate throughout the campaign. He's calling for sweeping out the old administration, meaning his opponent, and he's found some traction. Alas, many of the residents have bought the lies and are ignoring the facts.

"In the council race, the Planning Commission member is a woman, and as 57% of the voters are women, so she is a shoo-in, as the Americans say. The hotelier has been popular and visible in Carmel-by-the-Sea for 20 years. Their opponents are viewed with considerably less favor."

"It seems set, Holmes. Why did you decide to come all this way?"

He looked at me with his penetratingly sharp eyes. "Watson, I'm feeling a tremor in the universe. The Force is disturbed. While it is most apparent on the national stage, I believe that what happens in this local election will possibly be a bellwether, not just for the country but for the Western World."

"That is very broad, Holmes."

"Perhaps it is, but I am afraid we shall see that I am correct. I recall to you the book by Drew Westen titled **The Political Brain**. I listened to an interview our colleague, Tony Seton, did with Westen in which he asked if he was truly asserting that 95% of the voters chose on the basis of how well they liked or disliked a candidate rather than on the issues. Westen replied that it was probably 96%."

I shivered. "Not a good omen."

"No it isn't, especially here for Carmel-by-the-Sea

where the qualified candidate isn't as personable as his opponent, who trades on his hail-fellow-well-met personality – and his lies – to draw support from the others who have grown up in the village. Perhaps I shouldn't say 'grown up' since there is not an inkling of maturity among his supporters. Especially this candidate himself. He has a most questionable reputation, especially where women are concerned, treating them as he might have in high school."

I harrumphed again. "But I thought this was a very cultured village?"

"Yes," Holmes said in an airy voice, and he left it there.

The next morning, we strolled the few blocks to the post office, which is where the candidates spent considerable time during the last month of the campaign, meeting and greeting, handing out buttons and flyers. There were four candidates by the main door, and we dutifully collected their hand-outs. Several of them, when they heard our accents, displayed an immediate disinterest in us.

Then we walked across the street to where two other candidates were greeting people coming from the post office parking lot. They were clearly making an effort not to be in people's way. One of them was the always upper scale mayoral candidate. Rather than dismiss us for our not being voters, he engaged us about London and what recent theater we might have seen. A bright fellow, gracious, who no doubt would make a good mayor.

The other man was friendly and polite. When he introduced himself as Bobby Richards, I was taken somewhat aback and asked him what he was doing out of uniform. He looked at me curiously. Holmes laughed and explained, "My dear Watson, Bobby is the man's name. Short for Robert." And to Bobby he explained that 'bobby' was a term in England for a policeman. That cleared up, Holmes asked Bobby how his campaign was going.

"Mr. Holmes, it's hard to tell. Here we have absentee ballots sent out a month before the election, and many of the voters fill them out and send them in shortly after they arrive. Of course we don't see the results until they are counted on election night."

"That seems rather foolish," I blustered. "Situations can change in a month, surely. How might people change their votes if they chose to?"

The candidate looked at me in surprise, again. "Well, they can't, you know."

"It is a serious flaw in the American election system," Holmes explained. "They think they are making it easier for people to vote so that more of them will cast a ballot. But instead of making it easier, it becomes more muddled."

"Why should it be easier?" I demanded. "America is so proud of being a democracy, I would think people wouldn't need it to be easy to vote."

"Quite right, Watson. They might do better here if they did what they do in Australia, and that is to fine people who don't bother to cast their ballot."

As we bid goodbyes to the two candidates and headed back to the Cypress Inn, I sighed audibly. "I find this all very discouraging, Holmes."

"There is worse, I'm afraid. In a number of states controlled by Republicans, the legislatures have acted to make it more difficult for people to vote, requiring photographic identification on government issued ID cards."

"Why would they do that?"

"They say it is to prevent voter fraud."

"Voter fraud? Why would there be voter fraud if people need to be urged to vote?"

"Exactly, Watson. There is virtually none at all. But what they are really trying to do is discourage low-income people and minorities from voting. The barriers they are putting up will keep such people away from the polls as many of them don't have such identification."

I was outraged. "That's outrageous, Holmes. Surely they can't get away with such venality?"

"Sadly they do. The courts in America have been reluctant to intervene."

"Holmes, I think we should get away from this political miasma. When you've seen and heard enough, of course," I added.

"I share your feelings, my old friend. Why don't you perch in the living room with a good book this afternoon, and I'll get my fill of local politics walking the streets and listening in on conversations."

"You are a noble investigator, indeed."

And so it was that I spent the afternoon with Thomas Franks' book, *Listen, Liberal: Or, What Ever Happened to the Party of the People?*, and enjoying high tea before the fireplace. My friend returned late in the day, a discouraged look on his face. I knew better than to ask him what he had learned, knowing that he would share with me what he had discovered at an appropriate time.

The next morning we drove our hired car to San Francisco where we wound up spending several days. We saw our first baseball game featuring the home team Giants, took a boat ride over to Alcatraz Island where we had a tour of the old prison, rode the cable car, and took in the impressive Palace of the Legion of Honor. We also spent many hours walking along the waterfront, through Chinatown – noting both the differences of and the similarities to what we had in London – and then by the shops at Union Square.

Not wanting to return to Carmel-by-the-Sea right away, I instead drove us up through Napa County, seeing the vineyards in beautiful spring bloom and tasting many local wines. We discussed driving to Los Angeles to see Hollywood but thought the trip would be too taxing. So we drove to Mendocino and saw where many of the exterior shots of the ***Murder, She Wrote***, one of Holmes' favorite television shows, were filmed.

Finally, we returned to Carmel-by-the-Sea, two days before we were to leave for home. The timing was excellent. Not only were we refreshed and looking forward to getting back to London, but we arrived back in the village the day after the election. We knew of the results before we started down the coast that morning and took some solace that at least Bobby Richards had done well.

"We must be of good cheer, Holmes," I instructed my passenger. "Perhaps the new mayor will grow into the job." Holmes "mmm'd" and that's where we left the discussion of politics.

Back at the Cypress Inn, we found an invitation from the gasogene (the top official) of the Diogenes Club of Carmel-by-the-Sea, the local Sherlockian association, inviting us to be honored guests at their bi-monthly black-tie dinner the next night. We regretted to him that we hadn't brought formal wear, but he pooh-pooh'd our situation as a triviality and we accepted the invitation. It was a glorious affair, at which we were greeted warmly and grandly celebrated, Holmes especially, as he should be.

The following morning we drove to the Monterey airport, turned in our car, and rode the short flight to San Francisco.

I confess that I felt a deep sigh of relief as Holmes and I boarded our plane for London, and then just as we were settling into our first-class seats, who should make himself known to us by speaking through the space between our seats but Holmes' older brother, Mycroft.

"Hello, gentlemen. I thought I might see you here."

I expressed my surprise in several wordless sounds, but Holmes tilted his head slightly toward the gap in the seats and said to his brother. "I was afraid your connection might be delayed, and that you wouldn't be able to join us."

"The commercial flight was delayed, but arrangements were made for me to come down in the governor's jet."

"Always wise to have a back-up," the younger brother observed drily. "And how is Moonshine?"

"Holmes," I insisted, "Moonshine is home-brewed alcohol."

"Yes, Watson, I know. It's a private joke. Something his father the former governor said about his son the governor."

"Actually, Sherlock, the nickname is Moonbeam because the son is seen as rather spacy; New Age, as it were. But he's fine, of course," Mycroft explained. "Though he doesn't let much reality into his bubble."

"Mmm," intoned his brother, knowing there was a second shoe to drop.

"His wife and political advisor, Anne, showed some distress about the national scene. She thinks Trump can out-poll Clinton."

"Good gracious!" I ejaculated. "Is that possible?"

"Calm yourself, Watson," Holmes said in his familiarly soothing voice. "Remember that America has that archaic electoral college system. In 2000, Gore out-polled Shrub, but still lost because of the Florida hanging-chad scandal. Clinton could lose the popular vote and Trump would still lose the election."

I breathed a noisy sigh of relief, though I was far from fully mollified. "What has happened to this country that such a rude, brutal, ignorant cretin could even be a candidate, let alone find a following?"

"You praise him with faint damns, my friend. He is far more dangerous than he seems."

"How is that possible?"

"You said it yourself. He has a following. It is not one man, but a third of this once-great nation that wants him to be president."

"But why? Don't they have any idea what Trump could do to this country? To the world? He won't forswear the use of nuclear weapons. He denigrates entire cultures, including America's neighbors. Three-quarters of all his campaign rhetoric is proven false. Why do they sanction such ideas?"

Mycroft spoke in a quiet voice, "My good doctor, perhaps you don't remember Calhoun's study of rat populations in the late 1950s. The over-population of rats produced self-destructive behavior and severe societal breakdown."

I remembered having studied Calhoun's experiments in medical training, and it took but a moment to draw the answer to my question out of his comment.

My friend extrapolated, "The Earth is five billion over-populated with human beings, Watson. It has meant a loss of income, the destruction of the American middle class, and the fraying of the public agreement such that the infrastructure isn't maintained, institutions are imploding, and corruption is eroding government at virtually all levels."

"You might add," said his brother, "that the desperation these circumstances have generated has pushed a large part of the population to choose religion as a haven from scientific truths. It is a suicidal path stretching out before most of Western civilization."

There wasn't much to be said after that and we settled back in our seats. The captain prepared us for our departure and I into a gloomy silence. The flight attendant plied us with glasses of champagne and the three of us downed half of a bottle before the plane reached our take-off position. Our silence continued until we reached cruising altitude, where and when I suddenly was struck by a notion.

"Holmes," I charged my friend, "this is why you wanted to come to Carmel. You saw it as a litmus test for America."

"Bravo, Watson. How clever of you!" There was only the slightest tinge of sarcasm in his tone.

"Well, I say, Holmes," I coughed slightly, "I was not fully convinced of your explanation of the purpose for this trip to Carmel-by-the-Sea." I was silent for a moment. "I must infer that the results there were discouraging for you. That they auger ill for the national vote in November."

My esteemed friend cocked his head and looked at me with a far-away, thoughtful gaze. "They could, Watson. Yes, they could. Regardless of who might be elected. If not the specific results of this vote then perhaps the next, since it would be unlikely that America would see significant change in the way the government is run and the people are treated. It could be that the 2020 election could install a paragon of evil...a dictator using the worst in people to pull down the world's once premiere democracy and replace it with...with what I wouldn't want to imagine."

Mycroft inserted pointedly, "The elections are but a symptomatic response, my good man. The cause is the social collapse due primarily to over-population and the concomitant crises that result from it. Over the next decade, food supplies will dwindle dramatically, due in large measure to more violent weather destroying vital crops. Pollution will increase. The oceans will be out-fished to beyond their current reproductive range. These conditions create violence, and with all the guns in the world, plus chemical and nuclear devices, it might be better for the United States to collapse rather than continue to be targeted as the great Satan."

I sighed and closed my eyes. The champagne and the plane's droning engines put me into a deep yet fitful sleep. We were passing over the Irish Sea when I woke up in a sweat from a disturbing dream. I dreamt that the gossip website Gawker had featured photographs of Donald Trump in a love nest with Caitlyn Jenner.

We landed comfortably in London and were soon returned to our homes, Holmes and I in our rooms at Baker Street and his brother at his club. We all were busy catching up on our lives after two weeks away, and that and other business extended to the end of the year. We did take time out to get together with Mycroft to watch the American elections results be reported early on our morning of November 9th.

It was interesting to note that Trump chose Carly Fiorina to be his vice-presidential running mate; he said she made him look good. It didn't in the polls. He immediately dropped ten points. The Democrats suffered a major hit when Hillary Clinton was indicted for obstruction of justice for destroying more than 31,000 emails on her private server. She refused to give up her delegates at the convention, even when her negative rating climbed above 110 percent. That didn't matter as the super-delegates jumped ship on the first ballot. On the second ballot the former first lady garnered the support of only three delegates; they were from Louisiana and had been drinking excessively.

Facing a revolt that threatened to destroy the convention hall, the delegates voted in their own best – indeed life-saving – interests to nominate Bernie Sanders. Sanders promised to serve for only one term, saying he thought he could get everything fixed by year four, and to prove it, he chose Elizabeth Warren as his running mate. They ran a clean, honest, sensible campaign and on election night, cleaned Trump's clock with the largest popular vote margin in the nation's history.

Everyone got together and sang *Kumbaya*. While heart-warming, it was also deafening, so few noticed another tremor in The Force.

Open to Life

You never know who will walk into your life, or you into theirs, literally or figuratively, but the odds of it being a significant encounter grow quantumly if you are open to possibilities. Call it kismet or synchronicity, you often meet people who will be important in your life if you view *running into* a stranger as being rich with potential. Such a *chance* meeting is even more likely when you aren't looking for someone.

This viewpoint is compounded for me because I am a journalist-cum-novelist. My imagination has a broad range. I see something behind the curtain in a simple news story, even when there is no curtain. While sometimes I am open to professional opportunities, the hopeful – not hopeless – romantic in me is always pleased to see a lovely woman – attractive rather than gorgeous; with a thoughtful smile and a generous spirit – who could be The One.

Of course, where one practices this open mind also matters. Tearing up losing betting slips at an OTB parlor, for instance, isn't going to generate a lot of important job leads. But plying a path by the ocean with a semi-purposeful stride, the stars could be ripe, so to say, to meet the next love of my life. And as regards this opportunity, let me importantly add, from personal experience, that she doesn't have to be alone. Her being with a fellow doesn't mean you are out of the ball game. He could even be her husband.

It was late August on a Saturday afternoon, and I was walking from Monastery Beach toward the mouth of the Carmel River. It's been a favorite perambulation of mine for years. Only a two-mile circuit, it features some of the finest scenery on the planet – ocean, beaches, forests, meadows, lagoons – and most people who walk this route know it already, and they are there less to see, and more to soak up, these marvels of Nature. I should mention the birds, too. Canadian geese (in season), ducks, scores of pelicans, hundreds of gulls, and various other specious are drawn to the area.

That day there was a couple walking ahead of me, strolling peacefully – read: more slowly – than I was. A man and woman together tend not to press on as quickly as does a regular on the path who is walking alone with his own mind. Our speeds weren't so different that I rushed past them; indeed it took some time to catch them up. As I went by, I turned my head toward them, and, by way of acknowledging them, announced with a smile that I wasn't stalking them. The woman said she had heard me approaching from the sound of crunching gravel behind them. We wished each other a fine day, and I proceeded on to the bluff above the river, and then around the bend to a bench that faced East, over the river, and looked down Carmel Valley.

Others might cross the sand that seasonally closed off the Carmel River from the ocean as they headed to the small parking lot that marked the beginning of civilization again. But *my* couple continued along my same route and came upon me sitting on the bench. I shifted over to make room and invited them to join me, which they did.

We chatted for probably fifteen minutes. Matt did most of the talking. Justifiably morose, he spoke about the trouble he was having with his insurance company, which was showing increasing reticence about covering medical procedures that he needed to manage a rare cancer that would kill him, sooner than later, if he didn't receive regular doses of a highly expensive experimental drug.

The drug, which had been in use in Europe for three years but was still "under consideration" by our own FDA, cost $15,000 for a shot, and Matt needed a shot every two weeks. That's $30,000 a month, $360,000 a year. The insurance company didn't put it that way – that it was a lot of money to keep a dying man alive – but suggested that Matt could do as well with only one injection a month of the still-experimental drug. They had him try the half-dose schedule, but the lab results showed that he went irredeemably downhill if the drug was stretched out.

Matt was a bright fellow, a now-retired professor who had taught macro-economics at the Middlebury Institute for International Studies. He was tired of battling the cancer and the insurance company, but the alternative was the reason why his spirits weren't higher.

Alicia, his wife, remained silent throughout most of our conversation. When I spoke, I looked at her to keep her in the conversation. She was an attractive woman. Her dirty-blonde hair was pulled back into a ponytail that came out the back of a baseball cap. Later I wondered what it would be like to be with someone you cared about for years and years, and the story of your marriage would never get better. As compassionate as one might want to be in such a situation, it would take a remarkably resilient person to stay upright, much less upbeat, through an incessant stream of negative news. I couldn't begin to imagine the thoughts that must have flowed in the quietest private moments of her mind.

Being a journalist who has always been interested in the workings of the human mind, I gave Matt my card and offered to interview him. About what? About his difficulties in dealing with our health care system, and also about how he was managing what he was facing; and the issues of life and death. He accepted my card and said he would think about it. Of course I hadn't expected him to be enthusiastic about talking about such things, but sometimes it can be useful for someone who needs to vent. On the other hand, his prognosis was really about little time or less, so there was nothing that my interview was likely to achieve for him; and little to be cheered about, by himself or my readers.

I was hoping to hear from him. Because, truth be told, as it always should be, I was hoping to see Alicia again. I don't mean to sound predatory, but there was something about this woman – a lot; not just appearance, which was casually comfortable, but the character beneath – that I found particularly attractive. No, I didn't want Matt to shuffle quickly off this mortal coil so that Alicia and I could be together for the rest of time. My picture was more in the nature of the three of us being together again; that she might decide it was time to have a life, and he would agree that she should. And I would be an integral part of that life.

Yes, I am sometimes spinning over-the-top romantic thoughts and that's why I write novels. But don't worry. My scruples and their hopes were not compromised by my interest in Alicia. I didn't hear from Matt, and I didn't know their last name or names. All I knew was that they lived in Pacific Grove. Too big a haystack to go hunting for a needle. And besides, if Alicia and I were meant to get together, the gods would show the way. They didn't have to look hard. Gods don't.

* * * * *

"Hi, is this Tony?"

I hadn't recognized the number in the Caller ID display, but then again, I'd never seen it before. The voice did not strike an immediate chord. It had been three months since I'd heard it before, and then it was only a few words.

"Yes it is..."

"My name is Alicia, Alicia Towne, but I don't think I ever told you my last name." She paused only briefly. "We – Matt and I – met you on a walk by the Carmel River."

The image clicked into my mind's eye. "Yes, of course, hello. How are you, and Matt?"

I heard her take a breath.

"Matt passed away two weeks ago. The cancer had metastasized...everywhere."

"I'm so sorry. I thought – he seemed to think that he had more time."

"Yes, that's what he said and that's what I thought, but I think he knew he was coming to the end."

"I hope it was peaceful."

"Thank you, yes it was. He made sure he had enough drugs so there wasn't any pain. At the end, he took a pill and just went to sleep. It was all his decision. He'd had enough."

"I would have liked to talk with him about how he managed to deal with what he did for so long."

"He talked about speaking with you. I thought it would be a good idea for him because he really only talked to me about his...his condition. I also knew that you were intelligent and sensitive, that you could evoke what was important. That you wouldn't sensationalize anything. But in the end, he didn't know how to tell his story without drawing sympathy – and especially not pity – which was something he didn't want to do."

Carefully I asked, "How are you doing, Alicia?"

There was silence on the other end of the line, "I guess somewhere between relieved and guilty." She laughed. "If that doesn't sound too self-serving."

"Not at all," I said in a strong voice. "It sounds very honest." And I added, "What I might have expected from you."

She didn't respond immediately and then asked, "What does that mean?" Her tone indicated surprise and confusion, and perhaps hope.

"Of course I only spent a few minutes in your presence, and you spoke very little. I mostly was talking with Matt, but I had a sense of you, that you were a very substantial person; you were someone of character."

She started to respond, but I interrupted her.

"Excuse me, but let me add that I thought it both noble of you, and sad, that much of your life had been about Matt and his disease. I hope this doesn't sound callous, but I hoped that the rest of your life would be joyous as a reward."

The ensuing silence from her end stretched over twenty seconds, and I had to ask. "Alicia, I hope I didn't say anything you might take as hurtful. I certainly didn't mean to cause you any pain."

I heard her take a deep breath. "Tony, would you like to get together?"

"I was hoping that's why you had called."

"Maybe we could go for a walk?"

"I think that would be a good idea. Did you have some place in mind, or might I suggest that we meet at the north end of Pebble Beach? There's a path by the Spanish Bay Golf Course, off Ocean View. You must know it....west of the Fishwife restaurant. Park by the side of the road?"

"And go over that little bridge?"

"That's the one."

"I love that path. I've gone there on my own a lot."

"Oh good. When would be a good time for you? I'm fairly open."

"Now?" I could almost hear her smile with that one word.

And she could probably hear mine. "I could meet you there in about eighteen minutes."

Alicia laughed. "Eighteen? Not fifteen or twenty?"

"Well, I think I could get there in fifteen, but I wouldn't want to keep you waiting."

"And not twenty because?"

"Because I didn't want to keep me waiting."

"See you soon."

"Right."

"And Tony?"

"Yes, Alicia."

"Thank you. I'm so glad that we met that afternoon. That you are who you are. It meant everything to me these last few months."

"Remind me to tell you...no, you won't have to remind me."

"To tell me what?"

"I'll remember. About how the gods will find a way."

"Eighteen minutes."

"Good."

Actually, traffic was light, it being only nine-thirty on a Sunday morning, so I was there in fourteen minutes. I pulled up behind the only other car parked off the road. As I got out of my car, the door on the car in front of me opened and Alicia stepped out. We closed our doors behind us without taking our eyes off each other. We stood for a long moment, looking at each other and then, smiling, walked toward each other. We stopped at the end of our cars, next to the space between that stood before the beginning of the path.

"You look very different, Alicia. There is a lot of light coming from you. You are, if I may say, very beautiful." Because indeed she was. Instead of an old parka over old jeans and her hair hidden under the baseball cap, she had on grey slacks and a dark turquoise sweater over a blue oxford cloth shirt. Her head was uncovered, her hair, parted in the middle, fell down to her shoulders. Most important, was that her energy was bright and free.

I nodded my head in the direction of the path and we moved toward it together. She slipped her arm through mine, keeping her eyes on the path before us. "I didn't look my best then. I was mostly just hanging on. I was trying to keep my energy up, for Matt's sake."

"I think it is an unfortunate myth that we could always do more in such circumstances. I think mostly we push our own personal envelope ever harder. At least that's true of the good people. Maybe the not-so-good as well. Maybe everyone is doing the best they can, and some people just can't do very well. If that makes any sense."

She squeezed my arm with hers. "So what's this you were going to tell me about how the gods will find a way. I've been on pins and needles for I don't know how many minutes now, waiting for you to tell me."

I took a long deep breath and let it out.

"Of course, you don't have to tell me, now, if it isn't the right time or something."

"No, it's the right time. Your candor removes any thought, if there was one, of holding back anything from you." And I told her of my thoughts during and subsequent to meeting her, with Matt, three months earlier. And I told her how I had left it in the hands of the gods if she and I were to be together.

She craned her face toward the sky and pronounced "Thank you" to the gods. I looked up as well and added, "Yes, thank you."

We walked in silence, crossing the little bridge over the trickle of a stream that in two months would carry off the winter rains. We passed by a plot of grass where the groundskeeper grew sod for the golf course. And then up a slight slope to the top of the dunes that edged the beach and then the Pacific. The sky was blue, the air still, the waves gently playful with the sand. A thick marine layer sat several miles offshore.

"Would it have been better if we had known then about today?" I asked.

She shook her head confidently. "I wouldn't have been

able to wait, Tony. It was only the uncertainty that made not seeing you possible. When Matt was at the doctor, I found your card and I memorized your phone numbers. And when the *Pine Cone* came out every Friday, I would open it to the back to read your article. When you stopped writing for them, I was worried that maybe you'd found something elsewhere and moved away." She shook her head, "But I happened to see you walking to your car at Trader Joe's, the one on Forest, with two bags of groceries and I knew that you weren't going anywhere." Alicia walked on a number of paces and then asked, "What about you?"

I chuckled. "I would like to say that I put my trust in the gods, that I exercised Jobian patience, but the fact was, I didn't have any choice. I hoped some time I would run into you, but that thought was mitigated by the concern of how I would behave. You would be with Matt, and I would be afraid of being transparent before him. Or if you were alone, my knees would shake and that would put you in an untenable position."

"So you knew how I felt about you?"

"I didn't think in those terms."

"Really? That's all I thought about. I tortured myself with my desire for you and my dread that I was deluding myself. That there was no basis in fact for what I was thinking."

"Ow. Sorry."

Alicia laughed. "My dear Tony, it was nothing you did, or could have done anything about it. It was all in my head."

"Apparently it wasn't just in your head alone."

"No. No, it wasn't." She raised her eyes from the path to me and smiled. "I must have known that, and my mind games were just to prevent me from trying to do something about it, or going mad."

In a gentle voice, resonant with feeling, I told her, "I'm glad you didn't go mad, Alicia."

She nodded her head and smiled. "When I spoke to you on the phone this morning, when you were right there for me – as though we'd only been away from each other on a trip or something – I knew what I had gone through was worth it. I knew, Tony. Hope was gone because you were there. Just as I had wanted you to be."

We stopped and turned to face each other. "I have taped to the bottom from of my computer screen a fortune from a Chinese fortune cookie. It's been up there for seven years. And I don't think I've read it since I put it up. Which is kinda silly since I put it up as a watchword for myself. When I got off the phone with you – what, less than an hour ago? – I was about to get up from my desk when it caught my eye. It reads, 'Trust – Your life has divine purpose. Trust that your path is unfolding as it should...in divine time, not yours.'"

"Wow. How timely, so to say."

We laughed.

"And it says to me, dear Alicia, that we don't have to make up any 'lost' time." It's all before us."

"Oh, I like that, Tony." She threw her arms open and took a deep breath of the ocean-fresh air, and then let it out in a long whoosh.

"Feels good, doesn't it?"

"It sure does."

"And it's more than a feeling of relief, isn't it?"

"Yes, much more."

"And no guilt?"

"And no guilt." She laughed. "That's all in the past. Somehow, miraculously part of the past, eons ago from the now. There are no footprints on the beach in front of us. No path to follow."

"Maybe one path," I offered.

"And where might that lead us?"

"How 'bout up to Spanish Bay?" I suggested. "Maybe we could get some brunch. If you're hungry."

"I'm ravenous, dear Tony. I couldn't eat this morning, waiting to call you." She took my hand and we walked toward the path.

We walked up to *Sticks,* and it being on the early side for many of the Spanish Bay guests, we had no trouble getting a window table that was as almost as close to Nature as was our walk. I held Alicia's chair as she sat down, and her look up at me glowed with appreciation at this treatment. The table was set for me to sit across from her, but as I moved to that chair, she was pulling the silverware and napkin around to the adjoining seat, which I gladly occupied.

"I know it's only been an hour since we began this – or maybe it was months ago – and there's so much to talk about, but I must tell you that I feel like I know you. Is that possible?"

"Past lives, or something? And by the way, I share your feeling. It's breathtaking. Amazing. So right."

We sighed together giddily and laughed again.

A waiter arrived with the menus. I beckoned him to bend over and whispered something in his ear.

"Yes sir," he said and disappeared. Alicia's smile had disappeared.

"What?" I asked gently. "I'm your best friend. You can say anything."

The smile returned. "It's just been so long that I was happy. It's new for me."

"Get used to it," I told her.

"Yes. It's not like it was wasted. It was so important

being supportive to Matt, but it was like I wasn't living my own life."

"I'm glad that you said that."

"Why?"

"Because when I thought about you after we met, I thought about the sacrifice you were making, and how important it would be after it was over for you to discover yourself. Not again, because you would be different, but without pre-conditions. This time, just for you."

Tears showed in her eyes. "I've missed you, Tony." Then she laughed and the tears slid down her cheeks. She made no move to dry them.

"Those tears look good on you, Alicia. Healthy, bright, promising."

She shook her head, smiling. "How do you so know the right words?"

"Because I don't have to think. They come through me."

The waiter returned, and while Alicia wiped away the tears, he put down two flutes in front of each of us, and then a split of Roederer Estate Brut. "I'll open it, thank you," I said to the waiter, "and please come back in ten minutes for our order." He nodded to me and left.

I started with the bottle. Alicia was about to ask about

the four glasses, but I pre-empted her by saying, "I didn't order a whole bottle because I thought we probably should keep our senses about us, at least through the morning."

She laughed. "Good idea."

Again she was about to ask about the glasses but demurred, watching as I poured a splash into one each of our glasses, and half-filled the other two. I picked up the short glass and she followed suit. "This is to our past. Thanks to all those who made the journey possible."

We clinked glasses, and in a moment, they were empty. I sat still for a moment, and Alicia picked up her other glass, as did I. "And here's to you, Tony, who started us on this wonderful journey of happiness. And to me," she added with a coy smile, "who will match you smile for smile, hug for hug, kiss for kiss, love for love."

We sat staring at each other for maybe a half-minute, and then Alicia raised her flute to my mouth and I did to hers. Without ever breaking our eye contact, we sipped each other's champagne.

When our glasses were returned to the table, I said with a voice that had a slight tremble in it, "That was very neat."

"Yes, but I don't think we should continue on an empty stomach."

We shared another laugh and picked up our menus. "I agree we need nourishment, Alicia – my, how I like the sound of your name..."

"I like the way you say it, Tony. It's like you add a special quality. Some kind of new italics or bolding or something. Anyway..."

"Anyway, I was thinking that the energy at this table was reducing my appetite somewhat, and maybe if you're feeling the same, we could split a something, or get two things..."

"And have the rest later?"

"Yes."

"Together? Jeez, don't I sound a bit over the top?"

Alicia shook her head with a big smile. "Yes together, and not over the top. Yes, this might be mind-boggling but it really isn't. It might be implausible but it's fact. It might be impossible, but it's so real."

"Maybe because it's what we've always wanted and now we have it. In the past I might have shied away because I wasn't ready for it." I shook my head. "No, because it wasn't you. And now everything is right because it is you."

"Your words and your energy and particularly your smile are music to my senses. I know we're just zipping along, but it feels so right. Why should we slow down arbitrarily?"

"I wouldn't think of it."

"Very good," I told her.

"We'll seatbelt thinking in the back seat and enjoy the ride."

We ordered our own breakfasts and tasted each other's meals. We talked about our roots and families and hobbies and favorites books and movies. She was surprised and delighted to learn that I didn't have a television set, and she said she only used hers to watch DVDs.

We deferred to our hunger and the comfort of sitting together for going on two hours to finish our breakfasts. Then we went back out on the trail and continued our walk, heading south toward Point Joe.

Alicia stopped us and turned toward me. She asked, "You noticed, didn't you, that we finished all of our food? What will we do to keep this going?"

"Hmm, good question," I observed, rubbing my chin. "I could shave. I didn't have time after our call."

"I think you look very handsome with a day's growth, Tony. Maybe some time I'll see two days."

"Three days and my face can act like a pumice stone."

Alicia chuckled, "That's an interesting concept." She reached up and rubbed my face. When she brought her hand down, she took mine and started us walking again. It wasn't just a writer's imagination. We were a perfect fit.

<u>Dialectic</u>

Through the trees
Of whistling leaves
And creaking boughs
The heavens speak.

Through the brooks
Of burbling flow
And hissing rocks
The earth responds.

Through the voice
Of warbling tones
And parsing words
The mind opines.

Through the touch
Of glistening lips
And caressing fingers
The heart declares.

Through the marriage
Of trusting bonds
And dancing souls
The lovers grow.

Philip's Rotary Club Address

Phillip Hewes crossed the country, leaving a cushy position teaching English Literature at an upscale high school on the Maryland eastern shore to resituate himself in Redding (California) to teach English Lit at a two-year college there at the northern end of the Sacramento Valley. However, two days after he arrived, he was notified that the position had been revoked. As detailed in the novel, *Trinidad Head,* his life began with a road trip that proved to be the real reason for his transcontinental relocation. He was invited to speak before the big-dog Rotary Club to speak of his experience. This is what he told them.

As I replaced the Rotary president at the podium, it was to what seemed to be considerable applause. I hadn't known what to expect, but this was much better than silence and hostile glares that I once thought it might have been. It was clear from the look that I got from him that he was surprised, too.

"It is an honor to be invited to speak to such an important group. I know from your membership list that you are the political, social, and professional leadership of this community. From the numbers here today, and that warm reception, I infer that it speaks volumes about the hunger we all share that this community move forward." There was more applause. Georgette said that they didn't interrupt speakers like that...ever.

"I didn't know what to expect when I accepted the job at Lassen Community College. I was embarking on a new life, and I thought I'd be learning as much as I was teaching. It should always be such, by the way. There is a Buddhist saying that the best teacher knows himself to be a student, and in the 24 years that I have been a teacher, I have also loved being a student. I mean that literally, for I have not only better understood the literature about which I have instructed – books that I have read many times over the years – but I have, more importantly, learned about people, especially those who sat in my class.

"Thank goodness, because in the process, I have learned how little I actually knew. In the beginning, when I stood in front of the class, I thought that I was in charge. That the young people before me knew that it was their 'job' to listen and learn. That didn't last long. They didn't know that was their job." That produced light laughter.

"And it was then that I began to see those students...as people, as individuals. I say that with great humility, because of course they were people, but it was curious that it took some time to realize that they were human beings, not just names on a class list. It opened up a whole new world for me. Each young person was there for his or her own reasons, listening – or not – because they had to, or they wanted to be there in my class. Our class."

I paused for a moment and smiled at a recollection. "I remember taking courses in college where the teachers spoke from dog-eared notes. On the one hand I could appreciate that they wanted to cover certain ground, but there was that bit of doubt in the back of my mind that I was at all special to them. That maybe it didn't matter to the professor that I, or any of my fellow students, were sitting before him. Maybe he was just going through his course notes because it was easier than thinking a-fresh about what it was he wanted to impart.

"I could understand how people got that way, and when I made the decision to teach, I vowed never to take that approach. Seeing all of the students individually made it impossible to teach that way, as it also made it so exciting, enriching every class, to engage these young minds with the brilliance, the dedication, the grace, the power, of some of the finest writing of our civilization.

"It was my purpose to share the awe of what the human mind is truly capable of producing. After all, isn't that why we are here? To explore what we can do? To live a life that is a legacy in itself? To pass on from this life having left our community, our world, better for our having been here?

"Why did I leave a comfortable position in a beautiful area of Maryland? Maybe because it *was* comfortable. Life should be more exciting than comfortable. In fact, comfortable can be destructive. You can turn your life into a habit. Consider that the average American household has a television on for 152 hours a month. Think of what you could do in 152 hours. You could learn a new language, how to play tennis or golf, or a musical instrument. And that's what you could do with the hours of just one month instead of watching television. And this goes on year after year.

"That wasn't my problem. I don't watch television, except some DVDs and old tapes. But I was feeling comfortable. Oh, my teaching was successful, but I wasn't learning as much as I used to. So after thinking of doing something different, I decided to do what I was good at, but to do it with different students in a different venue. I thought the teaching environment here at the northern end of the Sacramento Valley – with its hot summers, salt-of-the-Earth people, the mining and lumber roots – would be a great situation for me, to re-hone my edge, if you will."

Saying those words sharpened my tone. "I'll readily confess that when, two days after I had arrived here, I had found and rented a house, and was ready for the classroom, and a messenger in pink hot-pants handed me a letter telling me that the agreement had been uni-laterally canceled – because the administration had failed to consult with the teachers union – I was, shall I say, irked." There was some light laughter in the audience, but most passed on the humor.

"You've seen and heard in the media that my attorney, the esteemed Georgette Rutledge, whom many of you have had the pleasure – or at least the privilege – of knowing over the years, filed a $20 million lawsuit in my name against the school and guilty parties. And if it needs to be said, the suit isn't about the money. It's about making change at Lassen Community College so that the school puts its students first, and to ensure that their education is more important than petty rules and regulations.

"Who am I to come into this community from the other side of the country to stir things up?" I stopped and smiled. Then I continued. "I hope I am appreci-ated."

There was murmuring in the audience. "Of course none of this was what I anticipated. I came here to teach, to expand my horizons, and to enhance my skills. I expected that coming from the outside, my success would be measured by how the students in my classes enjoyed the learning process, and how many of them decided to go on to higher education, applying to better schools than they had in the past."

I took a deep breath. "I think it would have been

grand if it had worked out." I stopped again, looking down at my hands on the podium for what must have been ten seconds, though it seemed longer. Then I looked up and scanned the audience from side to side.

"Yes, it would have been grand." I took a breath and let it out and said, "I believe that's all I have to say, except, thank you, again for inviting me to speak, and for being such a gracious audience." I nodded my head, I don't know why, and then added, "I would welcome any questions you might have."

There was a stony silence for perhaps three seconds and then the applause started. Then people stood up and continued their clapping. The Rotary president came up toward me, stood back a few feet and joined the applause. Then, recognizing my discomfort with the display, after a half-minute, he walked up to me, shook my hand and took control of the room.

Yo

My friend Yo – that's not his real name, of course, but

I've never bothered to ask him what it is – sets me straight on a lot of things. Which is kinda curious, since he is as far from straight thinking as anyone I've ever met. He says the most outlandish stuff, but when I think about it later, it makes all too much sense.

Not to besmirch The Golden State but Yo was the first person I met in California who really made any sense. For a while, I just used to just pretend that I understood all that my-karma-ran-over-your-dogma jargon. There was none of that with Yo.

I met him during my early days in Mill Valley, when I first moved West from New York. I was walking along in the redwood canyon near my house, and I heard this loud voice call out, "Yo".

Not having seen any of the Sylvester Stallone movies, I responded in the direction of the sound: "Yo?"

Out of the bushes comes this strange-looking fellow who said, "Yeah?"

"Yo?"

"Yeah."

I was having a dialogue with someone who might have been the cross between the Scott Mackenzie's original flower child and an aluminum siding salesman from Secaucus. He was about my height, five-nine, and a little gaunt, maybe 140 pounds. But he didn't have that hollow look of a speed freak. He had neatly-brushed, long blond hair that came down to his shoulders, a blond Fu Manchu mustache that probably stretched six inches from end to end, and a wispy blond Van Dyke beard.

His eyes were cobalt blue – I thought he was wearing those new designer contacts – and his pupils were dilated to the size of nickels. It wasn't from drugs, he told me another time, or too much television; he wasn't sure why his eyes were that way. And anyway, he was able to see a bigger picture with them. From the lobe in each of his pierced ears hung silver rings with a dime in each. Emergency funds, he explained, in case he needed to make a call. (This was in the days before mobile phones, but I wouldn't have been surprised if today he would eschew such a device.) He used to wear only one, but then the phone company raised the rates, so he shrugged his shoulders and stayed prepared.

His outfit was a cross between Flash Gordon and Maria Shriver. I've never seen such shoulders. Wide and square, he looked like a David Bowie act from the Seventies. He wore an oversized bright blue-purple shiny silk blouse that fairly matched his eyes, and puffy pantaloons of the same material in deep scarlet. Separating these pieces rather starkly was a six-inch wide shiny white vinyl belt; it velcro'd in the back. And to complete the outfit, if you hadn't already guessed, were over-the-calf black motorcycle boots with silver buckles to match the earrings. In the almost decade that I've known him, Yo has changed the in-between, but the earrings and the boots have always stayed the same; I don't know about the only-presumed socks.

It took me a few dropped-jaw moments to take all of this in. "Yo?" I offered again, tentatively.

"Yeah?" he responded.

"What's up?" I asked, trying a slightly different tack.

"'Up' man?" He started shaking his head, and then his hands, which as they were shaking began to rise. When they had come up to hip level, his eyes caught sight of his hands and they followed them as they continued to rise to above his head.

"Birds," he reported, "and clouds. And oh yeah, stars."

"Stars?" I asked, following his gaze into the bright afternoon sky quite visible above the sides of the canyon. "You can see stars?"

"Well, sure, can't you?"

"No," I confessed, shaking my head.

When he saw that, his stopped his hands shaking and let them drift down to his sides. "Maybe later," he offered with a touch of sympathy. "Neat things, you know. You want to keep a look out for them."

"Stars?"

"Yeah. I was in Hollywood once, and there were lots of them."

I started to chuckle but stifled it into a cough when I saw in his knotting brow that he hadn't said anything he saw as funny.

"There are lots of them down there, and lots who are trying. But you know, if they weren't trying to do someone else's act, they might make it work."

"Makes sense," I agreed.

"I mean, think about it man, they all wear other people's clothes and sunglasses and stuff. And they walk like other people, funny; like they put on their little brother's shorts, you know? And they're always looking around to see who's looking at them. Well, when you see that all the time, who's gonna look anymore, if you know what I mean?"

Suddenly I was worried. This strange looking fellow was starting to make sense to me. Giving back what I knew about stars, I said, "Did you know that if you stood at the bottom of a well you could see stars even in bright daylight?"

Yo looked at me, waiting for more. I realized that he had already indicated that he could see stars and was probably thinking I was pretty damned weird for thinking about standing at the bottom of a well. "You know," he said, looking around to make sure that no one was listening, "I think people who aren't, you know, like you and me, might think it's a little weird to, you know, climb down into a well to look for stars."

He had leaned forward and lowered his voice to say this, and now he drew his head back and resumed his normal speaking level. "I'd just tell 'em you were having a reaction to your sinus medicine or something, if they asked. That's what my parents used to say about me if one of their friends didn't understand what I said."

"And did it work?"

"Work, man?"

"Did they buy it?"

Yo looked at me, reflected briefly, and then said, "There was nothing for sale."

And I understood what he meant.

* * * * *

"So, Yo?" I began when we'd stumbled across each other during another of my exo-depressive sojourns in the redwood canyon, "What do you think of capital punishment?"

"No, man, no. Absolutely wrong. I mean, I can get where you're coming from. Those guys are a bunch of greedy nincompoops, mostly. But you know, there are a couple of fellows and maybe a gal or two who are doing some good work, or trying. You can't just take it out on all of 'em."

I figured out our different paths in a really very short period of time. "No, Yo. I didn't mean punishing everyone who worked in the Washington." I paused because it was an idea suddenly enfranchised with a good deal of merit. But no, Yo was right, there were some good people in Our Nation's Capital.

I explained, "The term capital punishment means the state killing someone. The government decides that someone has been so criminal that they should be put to death in the gas chamber."

Yo started laughing, "Killing someone? Hey man, I can see sending someone who's been bad to the Gas Chamber; that's gotta be one of the hottest clubs in South Bakersfield for standup comics. Their stuff's a gas. That's a great idea, making the bad people laugh, cause then maybe they'll turn themselves around. It always helps to have a sense of humor. But you don't want to get the government involved, man. They just get in the way."

"So you don't think anyone can commit a crime bad enough for which they should be killed?"

"Like what man? All the bad stuff they get paid for. You ever watch television? Those people get big, big bucks to produce that big bad stuff. And how 'bout those restaurants where you don't get out of your car? That stuff they give you is real, real bad."

"I'm talking about murderers and rapists and people like that."

"And what, you think we should kill 'em? Hey man, that's crazy. They don't do that stuff cause they're trying to be bad. They're broken. They got their brains scrambled up somehow, maybe rattled by their folks or something. You take them out, and that's the crime."

"But what about the people they hurt, and their families? They want some kind of punishment. The people in the capital who make the laws say more than three out of every four people in this country believe in a life for a life."

"Well yeah, that's right, but what you're talking about is a death for a death. A life for a life is when the people like you and me take the people who are broken, and we get 'em fixed. That's better than punishment. You make it so they don't do bad stuff again, and at the same time you take the punishment out of the capital."

We could really use such thinking in government.

__By the Seat of My Pants__

This happened in January 2019. It was written for pilots but should be understood by most who have flown in small planes.

I had been flying mostly sporadically until a few years ago when circumstances reflecting the old adage that small planes turn money into noise suggested that I needed to make less noise. But at the end of August (2018), there was enough in the till and more on the way to get back into the cockpit. *Enough* meant being able to get in the air every two weeks or so to keep the rust off my "wings."

This was important to me. I had gotten my private pilot's license 20 years earlier, when I was 49, and it was one of the greatest accomplishments of my life. Now, a couple of weeks shy of my 68th birthday, I was ready to fly again. And I would continue to fly until I found that my perceptive ability or skills were no longer up to the task. I felt I had a good decade of flying left.

I went up with a pilot friend, Philippe Tourtin, a

couple of times for an hour or so, just to get back my feel of the aircraft, a 40-year-old Skyhawk available from Aerodynamic Aviation at Monterey Regional Airport. I needed my arms and legs to remember what I hadn't used them for in three years. We had a fine time, but I decided I wanted to fly with a CFI (certified flight instructor); first, to see what I hadn't been doing – right and wrong – with Philippe, and second, to prepare for my BFR (biannual flight review).

I was connected with a wonderful CFI, Tom Woodruff, with the intention of making sure I had buffed up the skills I needed to fly by myself. That's what Tom wanted to find out, too, of course. He had me do a couple of 360's that went so smoothly I surprised myself, and then I did slow speed flight towards a stall. I did so well that Tom signed me off after our first hour together.

However, we went out again ten days later, and he had me do an engine-out drill, before we flew to Salinas. A towered field with crisscrossing runways and very little traffic, KSNS is a great place to train and test. There I did some short-field landings and take-offs. Altogether Tom and I flew an extra five hours over as many trips for me to get more familiar with what I needed to know, and comfortable doing it.

During the first week of January, I flew my first solo. The weather here on the Monterey Peninsula was lovely. I flew out of KMRY, and on take-off saw that the oil access door was open. I told the tower I wanted to come back, and while they were ready to have me come back around, I told him I could fly back in the pattern. I brought the plane to the run-up area, turned off the engine, got out, made sure the door was down tight, and I was ready to depart.

My plan was to fly to Hollister, a short flight, only 28 miles which I would fly at 2500 feet. KCVH is not a towered airport, so it would mean that I would go from the KMRY Charlie airspace to NorCal ATC (air traffic control) and then to VFR (no ATC) when I caught sight of CVH. I would enter the downwind to Runway 31 on a 45-degree angle, make my descent, shoot a *touch-and-go*, and return to Monterey. It wasn't an arduous trip, but it met my intention of polishing various skills. There was no other traffic at CVH that morning, so I had no jostling with others in the pattern.

Two weeks later, I booked the same Cessna 172P for the same gig. The pilot's seat was loose but I thought it was locked. It turned out it wasn't, but that did not become clear until I was on the *go* segment after my *touch* down in Hollister. The seat slid back and my feet couldn't reach the pedals. I was at full throttle, and seconds later at 60 knots, I pulled the plane up off the runway and into the air, climbing to 3,000 feet. Then taking careful hold of the top of the panel, I pulled myself closer.

Once level, I tried to click the seat into place but it wouldn't take hold. I realized that I had to get myself over to the right seat, because I would, of course, need the pedals to steer and slow down when I landed at Monterey. I tossed my flight bag, which was sitting on the right seat, into the back seat, undid the other seat belt, and then, unthreading the headset cord which had somehow gotten snarled in my shoulder harness, released myself from the constraints of the unre-strained left seat.

I don't know how it got entangled but I took my time making sure it didn't get pulled out. ATC had had trouble hearing me when I departed MRY, and I had switched to my second radio. I didn't want to mess with the communications I had by switching to the right-seat headset connectors. Then I slipped over to the right seat, seat-belted myself in, and called ATC for the ride back to Monterey. I didn't tell them about the need to change seats – thinking there was nothing they could do – and the action would be when the rubber hit the road at MRY.

Yes, I know it would have been a good thing to practice, but I had not sat – let alone flown – right seat in many years. Now I had no choice. There was nothing I could do but relax and concentrate. But I faced another unfamiliar factor, and that was the wind, which was coming in from the northeast (which it never did) which meant I would be coming in on 10-Right. It wasn't a serious issue, just something else that was not familiar. I was handed off from ATC to MRY tower and headed west over the ocean, planning for a long final.

The best laid plans....et cetera. The first thing was to fly a left-360 circle before I got near the glide path to give time to a regional jet that was coming in for a landing. No problem; in fact I was pleased at how smooth I kept the altitude and speed. But next the Monterey tower switched me over from the longer 10-Right (7,175 × 150 ft) to the shorter 10-Left (3,503 × 60 ft), and warned me of wake turbulence.

Hmm, I thought. There was an eight-knot crosswind and I was far enough out that the CRJ would be long off the runway by the time I would touch down. I was not happy with the change. I told the tower that I had a mechanical problem and wanted 10-Right. I said I would take 10-Left if I had to but.... After thirty seconds he gave me 10-Right.

As it happened, all my "challenges" were well behind me. I made a good landing and taxied up the ramp to parking.

To veteran pilots, this may not seem like a big deal, but to me it was. I was pleased that I had dialogued with myself on how to handle the situation, calmly and effectively. It provided a feeling of confidence that had been missing, and probably why I had waited to solo. I'll be flying again in two weeks, probably in the same old bird.

Two for The Canon

This is the first from the series *From the Garden of Continuing Reflection*. It was presented before the Diogenes Club of Carmel by the Sea on January 27, 2001.

Two men walk to the center of the stage from opposite sides. They see each other, hesitate, and then continue walking. Then both stop and turn. They eye each other. SIR ARTHUR CONAN DOYLE and SHERLOCK HOLMES approach each other but keep their distance. DOYLE looks at two chairs near the front of the stage, and then at HOLMES, who promptly sits down. DOYLE sits across from him.

DOYLE: (hrumphs as he settles into his chair) I suppose it was inevitable, that we should meet. And appropriate that it might be before such an august group as this. (He gestures toward the audience.) And on Ladies Night.[1]

---

[1] The Diogenes Club was men only, but for much of its history, one of its six bi-monthly meetings was opened to the ladies of the members.

HOLMES: Yes, Ladies Night. I was told that we have to be more entertaining than usual. During the year, it's all right if the presentations put members to sleep, but not tonight.

DOYLE: I'll do what I can.

There is a brief silence.

HOLMES: You're not doing very well so far. (flashes a quick smile.)

DOYLE: (ignores the comment) I wondered who you would really be.

HOLMES: You mean, now that I am out from under your nib?

DOYLE: Something like that. (not comfortable yet.)

HOLMES: (relenting) I think you probably captured me pretty well. Or maybe I'm the result of your own strictures. (moves his chair slightly closer toward Doyle) Tell me, how did you manage me? I always felt I had a great deal of flexibility.

DOYLE: (laughs) You usually had a loose rein. Sometimes you would take the plot and turn in a direction I hadn't expected.

HOLMES: What do you mean, exactly?

DOYLE: I would start you off in one direction, and suddenly I received new pictures in my mind. (chuckles) It was as though you had a mind of your own.

HOLMES: (chuckles) I suppose I did at times. (sits

back in his chair.)

DOYLE : (fondly) You contributed mightily, Holmes. I never had a moment of writer's block. I could have written a hundred stories with you.

HOLMES: Why did you stop?

DOYLE: (hesitantly) I thought you were limiting me. (winces) I know that doesn't sound right, but let me tell you how I mean that. Because I've been thinking about it ever since Reichenbach Falls.

HOLMES arches his eyebrows.

DOYLE: It's like a reporter covering the same beat for too long. He gets stale.

HOLMES: (surprised) You felt you were getting stale? Writing my stories?

DOYLE nods.

HOLMES: I can't believe it.

DOYLE: Why does that seem so strange to you?

HOLMES: (softly) You always wrote so well. I can't imagine that it was anything but thrilling to write those stories.

DOYLE: (touched) Why Holmes, how good of you to say so. It wasn't that you weren't always scintillating, but I wanted to try other paths.

HOLMES: (bridling) Like Professor Challenger?

DOYLE: (gingerly) For example.

HOLMES: I ran into him the other day. I think he feels competitive toward me.

DOYLE: (dryly) Perhaps he was picking up the same from you.

HOLMES: I suppose that's true. I didn't really think that you needed to spend your valuable time on stories of dinosaurs, and the occult.

DOYLE: But you see, my dear Holmes, that was what I needed to stretch myself, internally.

HOLMES: (somewhat ruefully) Dinosaurs in the 20th century? They certainly are a juxtaposition from the deductive thinking you had me doing all those years.

DOYLE: Exactly my point.

HOLMES: Hmm. So let me ask you, what did you think of the movies that they made of your work about me?

DOYLE: (annoyed) My heavens, they were a disgrace to my writing and to your character.

HOLMES: (pleased to hear it) Especially the early productions.

DOYLE: Shame on them. (cools) Who was your favorites?

HOLMES: Basil Rathbone and Jeremy Brett.

DOYLE: Of course. I thought Brett did a good job.

HOLMES: You liked Brett because his scripts followed

The Canon so faithfully.

DOYLE: True enough, but the performances were also first rate. Much better than the Hollywood fare.

HOLMES: They didn't know better.

DOYLE: But you liked Rathbone?

HOLMES: I thought he demonstrated a particular acuity of perception - he was an aesthetic - though it was wasted on the scripts. I also liked his impatience.

DOYLE: And his pleasure when the evildoers got their just deserts.

There is a brief contemplative silence.

HOLMES: (adds) I sometimes found Brett a bit too effeminate, truth be told.

DOYLE: He did go overboard on occasion. He sometimes put more into the characterization than the character.

HOLMES: Well put. A little of the Freddy Eynsford-Hill left in him from *My Fair Lady*.

DOYLE: Aha.

More thoughtful silence.

HOLMES: You know, I always wondered why you didn't give me a love life. At least the occasional fling.

DOYLE: (cagily) You were always too busy with your work.

HOLMES: (not buying it) You gave Watson two wives – or was it three? – and even some romance.

DOYLE: Holmes, do you really think that you would have been able to accomplish all that you did if you'd had a love interest?

HOLMES: (mildly defensive) Yes, now that you ask. Surely you appreciated the electricity between me and Irini Adler.

DOYLE: Of course. I think that was more your doing than mine.

HOLMES: Well, yes, but it wasn't my idea to be the witness to her marriage.

DOYLE: (pleased with himself) I confess, that was one of the few times that I had to pull rank on you.

HOLMES: It seems to me I deserved to better defined in that area. Especially these days when homosexuality is such a public question. I mean, even Billy Wilder gave me a love interest in his *Private Life* movie.

DOYLE: But didn't he have her dispatched by a firing squad in Japan? Holmes, I can certainly appreciate your concern, but at the time I was writing about you, I thought I had rather filled up your life. Not only with the cases – both those Watson chronologued and the ones he merely alluded to – but there were the experiments and the monographs....

HOLMES: And the cocaine?

DOYLE: (frowns) And the violin. Holmes, do you think these were superfluous to your character? I don't see how you could have given up either the drug or the music for a love interest, as you put it.

HOLMES: (grumbling) I don't disagree that you filled my plate. But I wonder why you left me incomplete.

DOYLE: I am sorry, Holmes. It was never my intent to do so. (pauses) I am somewhat surprised that you did not complain about the cocaine.

HOLMES: Really? I thought that made a lot of sense. As I explained to Watson, "My mind is like a racing engine, tearing itself to pieces because it is not connected up with the work for which it was built." I only did the stuff when I didn't have a case. (shrugs) Today, however, cocaine is viewed so badly.

DOYLE: Probably because so many people abuse it, even though they do have "cases."

HOLMES: It's a wonder that I'm not some kind of pariah with the temperance-minded.

DOYLE: (huffs) To the contrary, you're the most popular character in the English language.

HOLMES: Too bad we can't collect royalties.

They laugh together.

HOLMES: By the way, when you had me go over the Falls with Moriarty, did you think you'd see me again?

DOYLE: You mean, did I intend to kill you off, permanently?

HOLMES: Well, there was all that publicity about my supposed death. Obituaries printed on the front page of newspapers from London to San Francisco to Bombay, and then Queen Victoria asking you personally to bring me back.

DOYLE: My dear fellow, I had no intention whatsoever that you should die. In Switzerland or *The Valley of Fear*. I just wanted to take a break. Besides, my wife said it made sense to put you on the shelf — her words — to increase demand.

HOLMES: What, in your mind, happened to me?

DOYLE: I thought I explained that when we brought you back to deal with Sebastian Moran. You traveled. I had you in Tibet. (smiles) I thought with some Eastern influence, I might find a nice blend with your compulsive Occidental mind.

HOLMES: What happened?

DOYLE: When I came back to you, I wanted the same old Holmes. I couldn't have had you say "Existential, my dear Watson," now could I?

HOLMES: (flashes another quick acknowledging smile) I suppose not. Though it does seem as though you might have grown me.

DOYLE: (shrugs) But I think you can see my point, about taking a break from you. I could write myriad cases for you, but as you always seemed to be at the apex of your profession, there were certain limitations.

HOLMES: Yes, I can see that. (cocks his head) You know, I never wanted to go America.

DOYLE: Holmes, in all fairness to me, I created a fine character in you. I gave you complete support, with your excellent flat about which you were never bothered about rent, the ever-faithful Mrs. Hudson, Watson, and the Baker Street Irregulars.

HOLMES: (chuckles) Today, I'm sure one of the tabloids would raise questions about me and those little street urchins.

DOYLE: (ignores the comment) I think you left the stage at just the right time. You will always be a hero, an exemplar.

HOLMES: Sir Arthur, about you. Did people mistake you for Watson?

DOYLE: (nods his head) Yes, actually, they did. They thought they were being clever. It was their obsessiveness over such ridiculous and small issues that, in part, drove me to ply other avenues.

HOLMES: I always thought there was another reason. By the way, was I based on your Dr. Bell?

DOYLE: Holmes, I'm surprised at you. Never has there been a more unique individual than you. You sprang whole from my literary loins.

HOLMES: (appreciates the comment; thoughtful) I've often wondered why you didn't imbue me with more of an ego.

DOYLE: More of an ego? Some people thought you were the ultimate egotist. I, of course, was vociferous in your defense. What they mistook as arrogance was...

HOLMES: ...impatience?

DOYLE: Precisely.

HOLMES: Bah! If I were an egotist, I wouldn't have allowed Lestrade, Gregson, and the others to take all the credit for what they might have stumbled over and still not seen.

DOYLE: It was all part of your perfection, Holmes.

HOLMES: (sighs) What did I ever do about money? Were my private rewards from clients and the government enough to keep me put up in such a style?

DOYLE: In my mind, you were an artist. You needed to be able to practice your craft without concern for such trivialities as finances. I always believed that you solved a case in your early teens years that produced the first in a series of grateful and wealthy benefactors.

HOLMES: So I earned what I had?

DOYLE: Oh, yes, indeed, though I also thought you might have created a significant trust income through the perspicacious investment of your fees.

HOLMES: (smile) I like that. It fits.

DOYLE: It does, doesn't it?

HOLMES: Might I ask you, what was the purpose of having Mycroft?

DOYLE: As your brother or your smarter brother?

HOLMES: Both.

DOYLE: Funny you should ask, dear fellow. Some people thought he was supposed to be me.

HOLMES: Was Mycroft someone to keep me humble?

DOYLE: (chuckles) There was that.

HOLMES: (pursues) And the real reason?

DOYLE: I thought that you needed a confidante. Not just the friend you found in Watson....

HOLMES: You mean the dear fellow to whom I had the audacity to say, "It may be that you are not yourself luminous, but are a conductor of light. Some people without possessing genius have a remarkable power of generating it."

DOYLE: Quite right. And you were right. That was his role. Someone to point to the obvious when you might, rarely, overlook it. But I thought you should have someone you could go to for greater wisdom. Who better than an older, smarter brother, whose realm was Whitehall and above?

HOLMES: So you think that your readers inferred that

there was more contact between us, Mycroft and me?

DOYLE: That was what I expected. Also, I think a lot of people wanted you to be happier than you seemed. Someone to rely on, to go to for help. And an older brother would be just the ticket, and not need further explanation.

HOLMES: I confess I took some comfort there.

DOYLE: Let me turn the tables on you, Holmes. How do you feel about the character as he appeared in the case stories?

HOLMES: What an interesting question for an author to ask?

DOYLE: I'm not sure that many writers would want to face their protagonists.

HOLMES: Probably not. But I was certainly pleased, for the most part, with who I was.

DOYLE: As a consulting detective?

HOLMES: More than that. As a human being. I thought you described me as a remarkably honest person. (considers) It probably would have been difficult for a woman to find such a character... (searches for just the word)...attractive.

DOYLE: (nods) That was my thinking. (peers) Holmes, what do you suppose made you such an enduring character? You are a paragon of western culture?

HOLMES: You mean aside from your brilliant writing?

DOYLE: (dismisses him with a wave of his hand) You define a profession. You stand for intellect and reason. You are the consummate private detective, on the side of good against evil, successful where the authorities fail. A true hero.

HOLMES: (smiles) I think I quote you correctly as having me say, "I cannot agree with those who rank modesty among the virtues. To a logician all things should be seen exactly as they are, and to underestimate one's self is as much a departure from the truth as to exaggerate one's powers." (clears his throat) I liked being me. I very much enjoyed the liberties you gave me to flesh out the character you gave me.

DOYLE: But what was it that so captured the public's imagination, and has for more than a century. (adds) Surely, there is no reason to think you will ever go out of favor.

HOLMES: My dear sir, I can only infer that you created my exemplary, if humble, character with your excellent mind and pen. You wrote the classic line about the dog that didn't bark. You enunciated the empirical truth when you said, "When you have eliminated the impossible, whatever remains, however improbable, must be the truth." You wrote of "the opalescent London reek," "the universal passkey of imagination," and my favorite, another explanation to Watson, "Education never ends... It is a series of lessons with the greatest for the last."

DOYLE: (flustered) Why Holmes, you honor me. Such as I have never known.

HOLMES: It is I, Sir Arthur, who was honored by your work. If I might express one regret, it is that too many of your readers were distracted by your plots to recognize what a fine way you had with words. (adds) I think one of my favorite passages was from the opening description in *The Five Orange Pips*. You wrote, "It was in the latter days of September, and the equinoctial gales had set in with exceptional violence. All day the wind had screamed and the rain had beaten against the windows, so that even here in the heart of great, hand-made London we were forced to raise our minds for the instant from the routine of life, and to recognize the presence of those great elemental forces which shriek at mankind through the bars of his civilization, like untamed beasts in a cage. As evening drew in, the storm grew higher and louder, and the wind cried and sobbed like a child in the chimney." That is very fine writing, and should be enjoyed and honored for as long as man shall love words.

DOYLE: (thoroughly humbled) Holmes, I don't know what to say.

HOLMES: Perhaps you've already said it.

After a long pause, the two men stand, bow to each other, and then to the audience.

A Letter to the Editor
(of various newspapers)

May 26, 2020

To the Editor:

It's curious how many people seem to find it socio-politically chic to describe themselves as running out of patience with the shelter-in-place policy. Especially since it seems to be saving many lives. An official report suggested that if the federal government had provided proper leadership in late January when the evidence became empirical, more than 36,000 American lives would have been saved.

But back to the free-fretters who seem proud to say that they've had enough. How clever they must think themselves to be, to smugly bluster their dissatisfaction toward the healthcare and pandemic experts who warn that premature association with others will produce spikes in hospitalizations, and more deaths. In fact there is clear proof in a slew of states, whose elected political officials decided to ignore that advice, with new high levels of the contagion, obviously not nearly under control.

The macho whiners who are calling for a reopening of

all that is closed are an ugly illustration of the degenerate nature of those fostering what may be a fatal schism in our country. For the polarization isn't about a difference of opinion; it is the starker difference between truth and lies. And underlying that posture is a seditious amorality that is wantonly tearing our nation apart.

Let them be reminded that their ultimate decision should be based on the obvious...that running out of patience is more manageable than is running out of breath.

Barefoot Gypsy Rage

Many bracelets clatter, clang.
Eyes narrowed to hard focus
    look out, see nothing.
Tight jaw, slack skin.
    Fists clenched, weight pendulously alert
    ready to attack,
    defend, enunciate.
Shoulders forward
    engaging, accusing,
Listening; only for the bait.

She stomps her rage
    at being held to this plane.
Her heritage, nomadic.
    Yes, mad-ic. Uncontrollable
    in a controlling world.
Emotions extolling difference,
    for their own sake.

Blend the great past,
    the wisdom, with now?

Say It Write

Anger holds sway in a
    ritual of exculpating dance.
Perhaps anon, you will
    allow the stormy child
The peace of grace.

(Published in *The Sunday [Monterey] Herald*, Sept. 7, 1986)

Jason's Treatise

Jason Isaac was on a mission from god. Well, not god actually, but some angelic creatures who gave him the power to see auras. Why did they do that? So Jason and his mate, Carole Holley – and The Dawg – could tell the world how the ability to see each other's auras could save the future; at least as it to the extent that most of them might actually live through it. Here is the information he was going to tell everyone. Well, those who could understand what he was saying to them.

The first thing that people must understand about auras is that they are a reflection of their true selves. A person is not his body but his soul. The body is a device to transport the soul.

The soul comes from a higher plane. You can see the footprint of the soul in images like Kirlian photography, an electroencephalogram or EEG which measures brain waves, or an electrocardiogram or EKG, which displays the heart action. There are other devices, too, but those are the obvious ones.

To get a picture in your mind, think of a movie with a hospital scene where a patient is on his last legs and a monitor shows a green line that pulsates with each heartbeat. When the person dies, the line goes flat and a buzzer sounds, summoning the emergency staff. That doesn't matter.

What matters is that when the heartbeat stops registering, it means that the energy that has been keeping the body alive – the energy that is the life of the person – has departed, and all that is left is the physical presence.

That energy made the heart pump, the lungs breathe, and worked all of the muscles so that they could move the body. That energy noted pain, and it repaired damage.

That energy was also the thoughts and emotions, the ideas and the hopes and dreams and fears. It was anger and love. It was the total uniqueness of the person. It was who they were. It was their soul.

That energy had arrived at the moment of conception, when the sperm and the egg got together. It is what grew the zygote into a full-fledged person.

That energy produced a personality to interface with the outside world. That energy is what we call life.

What you need to know as regards all of this and auras may already be obvious. The energy that is your life is quite visible outside the body's form. In fact, infants can see auras. It is often the reason why they react to people, positively or negatively.

But as infants become children and begin verbalizing, the very idea of seeing auras is taught out of them. Because their parents had learned not to see them since they were infants themselves, they taught their children that they can't see them. For many children, the assertion of not seeing auras is an important part of growing up. That is why children learning from other children wind up sharing their dismissal of seeing auras.

There are some cultures where auras are prized, but few in the so-called developed world, and not on a wide scale.

The truth is that auras can be seen by anyone. It's a matter of unlearning what they have been taught and accepted.

The key to unlearning is to realize just how extra-ordinary being human really is. And in particular, to understand that what distinguishes us from all other species are the abilities to reflect and to imagine.

First you need to reflect on the logic of auras. Think about the fact that it is your energy that powers everything about you, both your body and your mind. Realize that this energy manifests itself every moment of your life in a million different ways that you never even think about – much of which you take for granted – like all of the activity that keeps your body alive and well.

It's quite a system you've got working for you, this life-force energy. How your body functions is fascinating enough, but well beyond those physical mechanics is your character, which your soul energy has produced and refined to define your place in the world. It includes your dignity and integrity, courtesy and grace, your intellect, discipline, creativity, wit, and purpose. Or lack thereof. The degree of these qualities is apparent in your soul, and it reflects in your aura.

So just imagine...imagine what it would be like if everyone's higher qualities were visible to everyone else. You could tell how conscious people were. You could see if they were in fear. You would know if they represented a danger. Or if they were wise and direct. It would be clear if they were present or if their minds were stuck in the past or racing into the future. You could see if they were telling the truth.

That's the power of reading another person's aura.

Just imagine what a different world this would be if we knew where everyone stood. It may sound utopian – perhaps ridiculous to some – but this would be the next stage of our evolutionary development.

It would mean peace...as a steppingstone to the potential of the best in human achievement.

It would mean intimacy with power, if that doesn't seem too abstract.

The wonder and joy of living on our Earth with such capacity and understanding is beyond the horizon of our comprehension today, but it won't be for long.

Of course many people will resist. They have been living with their limited beliefs all of their lives. They have learned from a genesis of similarly-minded people that stretches back a hundred-thousand years.

Many people – most throughout the generations – have clung to religion to get them through their troubled times, and their pleasures, but in that process, they have been externalizing the responsibility for their own lives. But god is not outside of us. Our soul is the godhood within.

That's not going to go over well with many people certainly, but as more people expand their consciousness – and more people unblock their ability to see auras – then the tide will turn...in the direction of a healthy and productive and joyous future for everyone.

It will take several generations, no doubt, and at times and in some places, the ride will have serious bumps in it. That's understating what we might expect. But eventually everyone will be able to see auras, and we will arrive at where we have always been headed.

Let me offer some metaphors for the transition we will be going through.

You might conjure up in your mind two images of ocean divers. One is a scuba diver swimming not far from the surface in a wetsuit. The other is a deep-sea diver in heavy, clunky diving gear with a helmet and hoses coming out of it, plodding along the ocean floor. The skin diver, with nothing between his skin and the wetsuit, can swim easily. He's agile; he can turn quickly and respond immediately to what he might encounter, whereas the guy in the heavy suit is out of direct touch with his environment. He has to manipulate the suit around him to move, to act, to deal with whatever he faces.

So it is with our own being. That personality that the soul creates for us to get along in the world. If that personality is a thick mask or a shield that our soul uses to protect itself or to hide from the world, it's not so easy to function. But if that soul has made only a thin covering for itself, then he has a far more direct and immediate relationship with life around him. He's not playing games. He's not manipulating people. He's present and engaged. It's a far healthier way to live, at least in most societies, where we respect clarity and honesty more than we do an outsized ego.

An obvious move for anyone seeking to improve their position in the world is to reduce the gap between the personality and the soul. It's a process; it will take effort and some time, and it will almost inevitably alter your relationships. But the bottom line is that the greater congruity you have between your soul and the rest of the world, the happier, safer, and more powerful you will be because you won't have to pretend, play games, remember lies, or be someone different from who you are at your core.

You will have to be patient with yourself in this process. You will be shedding a skin, and that can leave you feeling vulnerable at times, but the fact is that the more of the personality that you shed, the stronger you are because you have less to explain and defend.

If you put yourself on this path, if you commit to the process, you will be constantly rewarded with truer feelings about yourself. You will have more energy because you're not having to carry the baggage of your personality, like that weighty deep-sea diving suit. You will breathe more easily. You will feel more present. You will be more alert to the functions of your own body. And ultimately, you will be able to see the auras of everyone around you.

Here is another image, one that might be useful to your understanding of how your mind works: Ideas come in through the right lobe of the brain and are translated in the left lobe. (I suggest that they come from the universal consciousness, or what Jung referred to as the collective unconsciousness, but the source doesn't really matter.) The translation is mostly from the language of the source to the language of the Earth, and how those ideas fit into your terrestrial context.

Over the years of your life, the left lobe has, in most cases, added editing to its translating. That's the work of the personality who receives new ideas through a filter of its own creation. You will certainly understand this if you give some thought to how you react to news or new ideas; it is with a paradigm of pre-set, customized expectations, attitudes, fears, and hopes, et cetera. You can make wonderful progress in expanding your consciousness if you make the effort to reduce the authority of your editor in this function. The more you can let the raw ideas come through, the more value you will find in them.

There is this important truth: The more effort you apply to this process of expanding your consciousness, the bigger the results you will see, and sooner. But you always need to look inside, not outside, to gauge your progress. It's like taking off in a jet. You are racing down the runway at 180 miles an hour and the outside world is speeding past you out the window. But when you have climbed to your cruising altitude and you look out the window, everything seems to be moving very slowly, even though in fact you are traveling at three times the speed you did at takeoff. So make the effort, but don't hurt yourself by measuring your progress by the response of others. Get your guidance from your own insides.

Understand that this is a larger challenge than changing *what* you think. It's about changing *how* you think. It's not about the inventory of your thoughts, but how you engage ideas...what you look at, what you consider or reject without considering, and how you make those choices. You have to shift your thinking habits, for they are only habits. You need to think for yourself and your soul instead of through your personality. The personality will resist; it will try to preserve its position. But step by step you can reduce the authority that you granted it and take back the power.

In this process you will want to reduce the number of external stimuli in your life. Turn off the television. Stop listening to talk radio. Only spend time with people you respect for their character; people who act with integrity. You might try meditation. Go for long walks, alone or with someone who doesn't require a lot of conversation. Reduce the general level of "noise" around you.

Also, if it has to be said, get yourself into good physical health. Don't use tobacco, drink little if any alcohol, don't eat junk food, and reduce your intake of sugar, caffeine, and other stimulants. Shift to healthy, natural products. And get plenty of sleep. Most people truly need eight hours of sleep; many benefit from naps. The healthier your body is, the better your mind will operate.

These additional observations...

– When people become more conscious, even before they can regain their sight of auras, they will always be aware from whence they came. That means they will never forget their roots, their earlier, limited consciousness. And that means they will never perpetrate violence down the ladder. All violence always rises from lower on the consciousness ladder, from people who don't know better. As you expand your consciousness, you can't imagine being violent toward someone who is less conscious. That does not mean, however, that you won't protect yourself; you have an obligation to do so.

– Most everyone has the potential for greatness; the ability to increase their consciousness beyond their current imagination. You should be aware that most people at the lower end of the social spectrum have been in a survival mode, and their first step in growing their consciousness requires that they let go of fear. The lack of security inherent in fear at the survival level can cause its own problems, and people need to be aware of that, especially the ramifications for families, clans, and tribes. The ability to read auras will enable people to recognize where there might be conflict and to avoid some of it. Very few people will listen, but here's the truth if you want to try: There is no use in being put off by the state of one's aura – yours or anyone else's. It reflects who the person really is, and it can't be faked. Increasing awareness and clearing out negative attitudes is the only thing that can do the trick.

– You will know immediately what the colors and other factors of auras mean when you see them. Their meanings are tacit in their appearance. There is no cause for worrying about misreading them.

– You may have already intuited that it is more important to focus on who you are that generates the quality of your aura, than to spend time checking others. There was a wonderful line in one of Douglas Adams' books in which a television anchorwoman was checking herself out in the mirror by the door of her hotel room before she went down to the lobby for an important interview. And as he described the scene, "She looked cool and in charge, and if she could fool herself, she could fool anybody."

This final thought. Back in 1985, Tina Turner recorded a very powerful song entitled, *We Don't Need Another Hero*. You might hold that thought when you consider that this next, critical stage in our evolution is about personal responsibility. As we expand our consciousness, we will recognize that we don't need another hero because we must be the heroes of our own time.

Cheerios, Oh No

Can you picture it? The huge combines scything their way through amber waves of grain. Gigantic red and green and yellow mechanical monsters plowing through seas of corn, plucking the ears from the stalks, and leaving a carpet of shredded husks where only moments, yet lifetimes, before golden seeds had reached yearningly toward the sun. In other fields, rivers of wheat and rye and barley foamed through the shoots into the hungry porters aligned to truck the fodder of those rending giants. And at the controls of these devastators are the men who chart the path of decimation. A new breed, born of the earth, co-opted by greed, fear, and the addiction to power to sit atop the mass of churning blades and lethal rumbling. Their arm-weary forebears were the hardy wielders of the death-delivering scythes. Today they ride unfeeling, enthroned in air-conditioned oblivion atop the murderous machines. They are The Cereal Killers.

Presidential Timbre

The second in the series of *From the Garden of Continuing Reflection*. This was originally written in February 2001.

BILL CLINTON walks hesitantly along the dock, looking at the names of the boats in their slips. He is looking for, the *Honeyfitz*. Not the yacht from Hyannis Port days; that was the *Honey Fitz*. He again peers at a piece of paper in his hand. He reads aloud, "Catalina 355. What the hell is a Catalina 355?" and more to himself, "What am I doing here?" As if in answer, his eyes come upon the *Honeyfitz*. He stops before climbing onto the boat. There is JOHN F. KENNEDY, looking as he did in 1963, removing the wheel cover.

Clinton: "Er, uh..." He clears his throat.

Kennedy is bent over, and when he looks up and sees Clinton, he finishes unhooking the cover and stands erect. "Come aboard, Mr. Clinton. They told me to expect you. Although I thought it was" – he checks his watch – "an hour ago. I was going to go out alone."

Clinton, uncertain of himself, steps down into the well of the boat. "Yes, sorry, I was delayed. Some paperwork matter. Getting the right directions."

Kennedy: (without acknowledging the statement) "Were you a sailor, Mr. Clinton?"

Clinton: "I went out on boats a few times...." –

Kennedy stows the canvas covers below and walks to the front of the boat where he unties the bow line and tosses it on the dock. He returns to the cockpit and starts the engine. He reaches behind, unties the stern line and tosses it on the dock. Then he sits on the cushion on the shelf seat behind the wheel and adds a little power. The boat begins moving out of the slip.

Kennedy: "Sit down." He gestures to the cushions lining both sides of the cockpit.

Clinton sits. He is clearly out of his element, and while putting on a casual face, it's clear that he is not comfortable with his circumstances.

Kennedy reaches into his windbreaker and takes out a cigar. He lights it. He looks at Clinton. "You like cigars, too, I seem to recall. Would you like one?"

Clinton shakes his head. "I think I'll see how my stomach does."

Kennedy nods, and returns his attention to clearing the marina. He seems in no particular hurry to engage his junior. When they are out of the marina, he gets up.

Kennedy: "Take the wheel, would you?"

Clinton gets up and moves behind the wheel.

Kennedy: (pointing) "Keep us headed toward the harbor entrance." He climbs up onto the decktop and unstraps the mainsail. He returns to the cockpit and starts cranking open the sail. The wind fills the sail and starts to heel the boat to one side. Clinton turns the wheel to keep his heading. Kennedy stands to the side, enjoying the view and the wind in his face.

Kennedy: "I love to sail. I don't think there's anything I enjoy more, in fact." He takes a deep breath of the fresh salt air. "And there's no pollution here, of course. The weather is always perfect, and there are never a lot of boats."

Clinton nods.

Kennedy: "What was your picture of heaven, or where you'd wind up after you died?"

Clinton: (grateful for the conversation) "I hadn't really thought about it. I didn't expect to...die...so young."

Kennedy nods. Clinton obviously didn't think about how old Kennedy was when he was shot.

Kennedy: "Did you think that you would go to heaven? Did you believe in heaven and hell?"

Clinton shrugs. "I didn't give it a lot of thought, as I say."

Kennedy: "Did you think you'd led an exemplary life?

One that would be rewarded, were there such rewards?"

Clinton (puzzled): "I don't recall that I thought about it."

Kennedy: "Let me ask it this way then, What was your driving force in life? What did you think your life was for? Was it about accomplishment? Were you just along for the ride? To try to have as much fun as you could?"

Clinton: "I wasn't brought up to think like that. Mostly it was just getting by, you know. Or probably you don't."

Kennedy doesn't respond.

Clinton: "You rich people, you forget that most people had to work hard just to scrape by. You Boston blue-blood Brahmans don't realize that you had an advantage that people like me never did. You had time to have a purpose. We were trying find enough to eat."

Kennedy: "It's not just about money, though. My father had money, it's true, but he didn't inherit it. He instilled in all of his children the need to produce. My mother was equally firm about our obligation to the public. She also imbued us with a sense of dignity."

Clinton: "Your point?"

Kennedy: "It doesn't seem, despite your obvious success, as though that lesson ever got through to you. Or to your wife, who was raised in higher circumstances."

Clinton: "Is this the sex thing?"

Kennedy: "No, sir, it's not all about sex."

Clinton: "What then?"

Kennedy: "It's about the way you finished out your presidency, pardoning people like Marc Rich, walking out the door with $200,000 in gifts, and then finding yourself office space in Manhattan that was going to cost taxpayers $700,000 a year."

Clinton: "That's not fair."

Kennedy: "What isn't fair?"

Clinton: "First of all, I didn't pardon Rich just because his wife had been generous to Hillary and me and the party, but because my pardon attorney recommended it."

Kennedy: "But he was Rich's attorney. Surely that should have warned you. And besides, there were plenty of people who were in federal prison who were deserving of pardons."

Clinton: "Like who?"

Kennedy: "How about all those women who were jailed on conspiracy counts under the drug statutes pushed through Congress in the late '80's for political reasons, and later amended."

Clinton: "I released some."

Kennedy: "A handful maybe, but not the thousands who shouldn't have been left behind bars. You knew better than that."

Clinton: "Well, I didn't have time to review all of the cases, and besides, we gave back half of the gifts."

Kennedy: "But not all. And some of them were clearly meant to stay in the White House. Don't you understand? You made yourselves look bad. You shamed the office by taking those things. It's not like you needed the money, for goodness sakes, what with your wife's book advance, and millions sure to come your way from your own book."

Clinton: "We needed the office space in New York, because Hillary is their Senator."

Kennedy: "But most past presidents are spending less than $200,000 a year on their offices. Surely you can appreciate how bad it looked for you to spend so much on yourself."

Clinton: "I thought the American public wanted to treat their ex-president well. I still have a lot more to contribute, you know."

Kennedy: "I understand what you're saying." He pauses. "Maybe it will look different to you later. But it was never about money."

Clinton remains quiet.

Kennedy: "I suppose it's easier to think about the esoteric things in life when you don't have to worry about your next meal, but as Lincoln said, by the time a man is forty, he has to take responsibility for how he looks. I may have been born into money, but my father drove us to be the best."

Clinton: "I was mostly raised by my mother."

Kennedy: "That's some of the difference, no doubt, but you were successful yourself at an early age, graduated Yale Law School, Rhodes scholar, Attorney General then Governor of Arkansas. Then President of the United States for two terms. Did you never stop to think where you were headed? What was the meaning of your life?"

Clinton: (shrugs again) "I guess not." (adds) "I was too busy."

Kennedy looks at him with an edge. "Busy doing what?"

Clinton (surprised, defensive) "Running the country?"

Kennedy nods acquiescently. "Steer a little to the right. We've caught the ocean breeze, and the currents shift a little bit up ahead. Make for a third of the way between the centerpoint and the harbor buoy."

They sail along in silence for a while. A variety of different expressions crease Clinton's face. Kennedy is contemplative.

Clinton: "I know that I'm dead, since I'm here with you, but I don't know how I died."

Kennedy: (between surprised and amused) "They didn't tell you?"

Clinton shakes his head. "What so funny?"

Kennedy: "What's the last thing that you remember?

Clinton: (thinks; eyes shift) I was visiting a, uh, a friend...."

Kennedy: "And?"

Clinton: "We'd had some pizza and were watching television."

Kennedy: (shakes his head) "You just don't get it, do you?"

Clinton: "What?"

Kennedy: "That the truth exists, even though you don't want to admit it."

Clinton: (bridles) "What are you saying?"

Kennedy: "You were having sex with a young woman when you suffered a heart attack."

Clinton: "Was that how I died? A heart attack in the saddle? Like Rockefeller."

Kennedy: "No, the woman with Nelson was 30 and old enough to know what she was doing. The woman – girl – you were with was barely 18."

Clinton: "Hey, John, you played around, probably as much as I did."

Kennedy: "Hardly, and I prefer that you address me more formally. We're not friends. This isn't about friendship. The difference between our behavior in this area is that I was discreet, and you virtually flaunted your promiscuity. I had relationships with adults, while you were flouncing about with women who didn't have the age or experience to know better."

Clinton: (chastened, but unrepentant) "I guess we'll just see that differently."

Kennedy: (evenly) "Mmm."

Clinton: (petulantly) "Just why am I here?"

Kennedy: "You're being vetted."

Clinton: "Vetted? Vetted for what? I'm already in heaven, aren't I?"

Kennedy: "Yes and no. You are where all people who die go. It's a wonderful place, and most of the souls who were bad people on Earth are here along with the good ones. They expected to go to hell, but very soon they understand the ill nature of their ways on Earth and they begin repenting right away."

Clinton: "So I'm here, then," He looks around him, "wherever this is. Why am I being checked out?"

Kennedy: (sighs) "Because all men who were once President of the United States are considered for membership in a private society."

Clinton: "And what's so special about this private society? Are there any perks?"

Kennedy: (smiles) "No, no perks. Nothing tangible really. Just the opportunity to spend time with some of the greatest leaders in history. Most of the founders – Washington, Jefferson, Madison, Monroe and Adams – and of course Lincoln and the Roosevelts. Others cycle through as guests every now and then."

Clinton: "Somehow I don't think you guys would want me to be part of your club."

Kennedy: "That's what this sail is about."

Clinton: (smugly) "Presuming that I would want to be a member."

Kennedy: "I brought up that point, but we have our rules."

Clinton: "So what if I don't join your club? What is heaven, or whatever you call it, supposed to be?"

Kennedy: "What would you like it to be?"

Clinton: "I don't know. I hadn't thought about it. (smiles) I guess I expected people to all have wings and play the harp. (laughs) Which doesn't sound very appealing."

Kennedy: "Mark Twain wondered about that description, too."

Clinton: (musing) "What would I like heaven to be?"

Kennedy: "I read that Paul Begala, one of your closest

advisors, said he thought you would have been perfectly content to teach law, and at the University of Arkansas."

Clinton: (laughs) "Until Hillary came along. With all her ambition."

Kennedy: "You weren't ambitious yourself?"

Clinton: "Phew. Not like her. She was like a moray eel. Even after you cut their head off, they're still biting you."

Kennedy: "Why did you marry her?"

Clinton: (a fresh thought to him) "I don't know. Maybe I thought she would be good for my career. She was from Park Ridge; she knew about society."

Kennedy: "Why do you think that she wanted to marry you?"

Clinton: "You know, that's a very good question. I think she thought she found a horse she could ride." (pleased with himself) "I think she thought she could go places with me." (pauses) "It really was her decision, you know. To get married, I mean. I was happy just to have her as a girlfriend."

Kennedy: "Exclusively."

Clinton: (with scorn) "Hillary? Would you?"

Kennedy doesn't answer. "I ask about what kind of heaven you might want because we never saw any real selection in your life on Earth. You didn't exhibit any real direction."

Clinton: (eyebrows raised) "Unless you count the fact that I came to the White House as a boy when I met you and rose to be elected president, not once but twice."

Kennedy: "Yes, you did, though Bob Dole was hardly a credible candidate."

Clinton: "The economy did well under my leadership."

Kennedy: "Please, sir, I'm not a constituent. You had as little to do with the performance of the economy as you do with cloud formation."

Clinton: "I supported Greenspan."

Kennedy: "And that's your idea of leadership?"

Clinton: "I could have mucked it up. Sometimes a true leader does nothing."

Kennedy: "Yes, of course. Please tell me, what do you classify as your greatest achievements in office? Domestic and international."

Clinton: "You can argue with me, but the economy...not getting in the way of it...and keeping the country on an even keel. When I got to the White House, the deficit was $250 billion, and that was about the size of the surplus when I left."

Kennedy says nothing.

Clinton: "Besides the economy, I put more cops on the

street and more teachers in the classroom. I would have done more, but the Republicans stopped me. Especially Gingrich, and Armey and DeLay. And then Lott."

Kennedy: "Admirable, of course, but American children continued to fall behind. Not only not catch up, but actually lose ground in the competition of the global economy. Test scores remain low. High school dropout rates are 30% in some areas. And many who do graduate may have a degree, but still can barely read. And they certainly have no real education."

Clinton looks resentful.

Kennedy: "And as far as crime going down, which is what I presume you were alluding to, crime dropped in large measure because the economy was heating up." He waits, but there is no response. "Race relations certainly didn't improve. The gap between rich and poor widened to the worst of any industrial nation. You did nothing about population growth, and barely preserved a woman's right to choose."

Clinton: "I did protect third-trimester abortions."

Kennedy: "Yes, you did, and it was a good thing, too. It was outrageous that the right-wing chose to make such a tragic procedure a political issue. And you did well to veto their legislation."

Clinton: "I also protected the wilderness. I preserved more federal land than even Roosevelt."

Kennedy: "You get very high marks for that, as well, Mr. Clinton. All of us – even those who have long been pro-development – recognize the benefit, and we hope that President Bush isn't able to undo what you have done. But why, we wondered, didn't you do more for the environment at the beginning of your first administration?"

Clinton: "I wish we had. They thought the gays-in-the-military issue would put all the conservatives on notice, and then we could implement our agenda."

Kennedy: "Which was...?"

Clinton: "Universal health care, for one."

Kennedy: "Why did that effort fail?"

Clinton: "Because I let Hillary handle it. She didn't even invite the doctors to her hearings. I can't believe her sometimes."

Kennedy: "Why did you leave it in her hands?"

Clinton: "She asked for it, and by the time I saw what she was doing, it was too late."

Kennedy: "What else was on your agenda?"

Clinton: (having trouble remembering) "I don't know, that was pretty much the first item of business. If we'd gotten health care straightened out, it would have been quite a feather in my cap."

Kennedy: "What about other issues? The Social Security system needs to be fixed. There is a housing crisis.

Old people don't have enough food or money to stay warm in the winter. A third of America's children are suffering from malnutrition. We rape and shoot more people than any other society in the world."

Clinton: (quizzically) "They were the same problems you faced, more or less, and everyone since, and no one did anything about them."

Kennedy: "Actually, we were getting started. I won't say that the Civil Rights Act was my legislation, but it started with me."

Clinton: "And passed over your dead body. No offense."

Kennedy: "If I had known it would take that, I would have made the deal. Is there any issue that you felt that strongly about?"

Clinton muses.

Kennedy: (reaching out) "I know that you are a compassionate man. I saw you moved by things that should move a man; like the Oklahoma bombing. But it seemed to stop, somewhere inside of you. We saw no passion. We didn't see any real purpose to you."

Clinton: "If the Republicans hadn't hated me so much, we could have gotten a lot done."

Kennedy: "What was your greatest disappointment?"

Clinton: (thinks) "My legacy."

Kennedy: "I beg your pardon?"

Clinton: "My legacy."

Kennedy: "I heard you. I didn't understand."

Clinton: "I didn't leave one. I tried to get a settlement in the Middle East, but Arafat – those Palestinians are really crazy – said he couldn't sell it to his people, and the Israelis seemed in a particularly hostile mood. They were going to elect that idiot Sharon, who is at least as demented as any Arab I ever met."

Kennedy: "Speaking of foreign policy, what were the high points for you?"

Clinton: "I think Kosovo."

Kennedy: "No regrets about not having stood up to Milosovic sooner? In Bosnia, or to protect the Croatians?"

Clinton: "I wanted to, but I was getting all sorts of conflicting advice. Some said we should let the Europeans solve their own problems. Some said it would be another Vietnam; we'd get in but we couldn't get out."

Kennedy: "So your policy was what, wait-and-see?"

Clinton: "You make that sound wrong."

Kennedy: "I wouldn't judge you, Mr. Clinton. But the fact is that the Serbs slaughtered, raped, and made homeless tens of thousands of people, under your watch."

Clinton: (angry) "And what would you have done?"

Kennedy: "I don't know exactly, but I would have stood up to Milosovic at the get-go. He's a bully, and unless you stop them immediately, they gather strength and are harder to stop later. If you had created a serious embargo – transportation, communications, and financial transactions – at the outset, the decision-makers in Belgrade would have forced him to back down."

Clinton: "Hindsight is great, but you weren't there."

Kennedy: "No, I wasn't. Nor was I in Somalia or Haiti, two other trouble spots where wait-and-see cost a lot of lives. Could they have been handled better? Probably, but you're right about hindsight. Perhaps the results you got were the best that could have been gotten."

Clinton: "You probably feel the same way about Cuba. And Vietnam."

Kennedy: "The Bay of Pigs was a disaster, and how that might have contributed to the subsequent missile crisis, I can only guess. I didn't do a very good job of sorting out the facts from the private agendas at the State Department or the CIA. I will tell you that I did not know about the Diem assassination in advance, and I was planning to get us out of Vietnam, regardless of what the revisionists say. That might have contributed to getting me killed."

Clinton: "Do you know about that? About your assassination?"

Kennedy nods. "Most of it."

Clinton: "Did Oswald act alone?"

Kennedy shakes his head. "I really can't talk about it. You can learn a lot about your own life, when you pass on, but not about others'. It's really none of anyone's business but those who were involved."

Clinton: "Will it ever become public?"

Kennedy: "I doubt it."

Clinton: "Doesn't that bother you? That people will never know?"

Kennedy: "It doesn't really matter, does it? Whether it was payback for CIA operations, or The Mob, or a rogue Soviet spy? What happened was that I was killed, and it moved the country in a different direction from where we were headed."

Clinton: "Why? Why was that necessary?"

Kennedy: "I'm not sure that you would understand."

Clinton offended: "Hey, I was a Rhodes Scholar, after all."

Kennedy: "Yes, of course." He clears his throat. "The United States had been defining global policy from the Second World War. From its position of strength, which wasn't also what was right. The country needed to learn more about itself before it could be a true world leader. That meant looking inward. Seeing the dark side of our power. My death opened the way to an expansion of the war in Vietnam – especially under Nixon and Kissinger – that cost millions of lives. It was wrong of us to be there. And that caused a lot of Americans to rethink power politics, the military, and war as answers. They're not, you know. Or perhaps you don't. But the truth is that if we can't lead by reason, then we are doomed to failure. And we must be right, too. Unfortunately, for so long, we have let the so-called intelligence community define foreign policy, and it has to often been in lethal error."

Clinton: "We're still the most powerful nation in the world. There's not even a close second."

Kennedy: "But that's based on fear. If not fear of our weapons, then fear of our cutting off aid. Or forcing other countries to stop trading with governments who don't toe our line. There are more than 30 wars going on around the world, and we are arming at least one side in every conflict. That is surely no way to lead."

Clinton: "What about you? What are your regrets?"

Kennedy: "That I didn't get to watch my children grow into adults. I'm so proud of Caroline, and John had grown into a fine man."

Clinton: "I mean about, uh, being killed. Not being president longer."

Kennedy: "It was never about being president for me, Mr. Clinton. It was about getting things done. Civil rights was critical, changing our foreign policy was another. Making sure that no child went to sleep hungry. Transforming schools from degree factories to centers of true and excited learning."

Clinton nods in agreement. "And you think those things can be accomplished? I mean, really? Not just campaign rhetoric?"

Kennedy: "Of course they can, but it takes character."

Clinton: "I know what you think of me, but what about Ford, Carter, Reagan, and Bush? Don't you think they were men of character?"

Kennedy: "Certainly, especially Carter, but it is not character alone. You need intellect and vision. You need courage and perseverance. Leading America requires a man who is more concerned with results than politics, solutions than his re-election."

Clinton: "Do you think you would have been re-elected? If you hadn't been shot?"

Kennedy: "Probably. I wasn't perfect in the job, surely, but I represented moving forward."

Clinton: (almost sneering) "Camelot?"

Kennedy: "Perhaps. For all that has been written since, the fact is that Jackie and I were young and vibrant. We had young children. We looked like the future, especially after General Eisenhower. We were about what was possible."

Clinton: "Not quite me and Hillary."

Kennedy: "No."

They are silent for a while.

Kennedy: "What was it that induced you to get involved with people like Paula Jones, Gennifer Flowers, and Monica Lewinsky and the others? Was it just sex? Was it the risk of getting caught?"

Clinton is about to answer but thinks better of it. Finally he speaks. "It wasn't the sex. I never had good sex, not with any of them. Maybe it was about risk. I needed boundaries, and there weren't any."

Kennedy: "You didn't feel bad about cheating on your wife?"

Clinton scoffs. "On Hillary? She knew all about what was going on, and she knew it before we were married. I think I played around sometimes just to rub her nose in how little she gave me. Not sexually, but as a woman. She wouldn't have jeopardized her future, and she saw me as her ticket."

Kennedy: "But you seemed to treat women badly as a rule. You assaulted Kathleen Willey in the White House. And more than the sexual misbehavior, you left Zoe Baird, Kimba Woods, Lani Guinier, and Jocelyn Elders all 'twisting slowly, slowly in the wind'. Did you feel no sense of remorse? Is there no chivalrous part of you?"

Clinton: (angry) "What about you? You cheated on your wife."

Kennedy: "Yes, I did. It was a different time, and a

different culture in some ways. But I don't offer any excuses. It seemed then that it was one of the accoutrements of power. If it hadn't seemed so acceptable at the time, I would feel even more ashamed than I do today. I didn't treat Jackie well."

Clinton: (cooler) "So what else do you want to know about me?"

Kennedy: "I don't know that it's fair to burden you with this, but some of the men wonder if you recognize the potential you had when you came to office. There was so much that needed to be done, and you were about to ride a strong economy for the rest of your terms."

Clinton: "I don't agree. There wasn't really that much potential. I wanted to accomplish things, you know, health care, education, crime. But it seemed like nothing worked. The Republicans wouldn't cooperate, and the Democrats mostly were interested only in their own re-election. It seemed like no one really wanted to get anything done. They were content with small changes and band-aids, anything they could take back to the voters."

Kennedy: "What were your plans, had you not died when you did?"

Clinton laughs. "I hadn't really thought about it. Hillary and I were going to separate. Quickly, so it wouldn't affect her chances of running for president in '04. I was content to lecture, travel, meet with friends."

He pauses and reflects. "I think I would have headed to Hollywood. I had a lot of friends out there, people who respected me. Even though I couldn't practice law for five years, I'm sure they could have lined up some consulting jobs for me. And I could have written my memoirs."

Kennedy: "Where do you think the country is headed?"

Clinton: "Under Bush?"

Kennedy: "And beyond."

Clinton: "I'm afraid that Bush is going to be a disaster. It's really Cheney who's running things, and he opposed choice, gun control, school lunch programs. We can only hope that the stress of running the country causes his heart to give out." Thinks about what he's said. "I don't mean that in a negative sense; about what's best for the country."

Kennedy: "So you think that Bush will be a one-term president?"

Clinton: "Oh, sure. There will be a honeymoon period, and once people get a good look at him, and at Cheney, they'll realize they've taken a step backwards."

Kennedy: "What would a step forward look like to you?"

Clinton: "Health care reform, for one. Get the insurance companies out of the picture."

Kennedy: "But you didn't go after that yourself?"

Clinton: "My advisors told us we couldn't get it, so we didn't go after it."

Kennedy: "Do you think Hillary will win?"

Clinton: "There are a lot of people who like her, and a lot of people who don't. I don't know. We'll have to see what happens with Bush."

Kennedy: "You don't think Gore will run again?"

Clinton: "Oh, goodness, no. He doesn't have the character for it. I mean, you must have seen, even from up...here, that he lost the election. He gave it to Bush in the debates when he came off like such an elitist wimp. All he had to do was be a little humble, but it's not who he is. And, poor guy, he can't fake it."

Kennedy: "You make it sound like he would have been a terrible president."

Clinton: "You may not have much respect for me, Mr. Kennedy, and history may judge me as not one of the best presidents, but I was a leader and a good one. I had some of the highest ratings of any president when I left office. That must mean something."

Kennedy: "What do you think it meant? I ask because you haven't listed many accomplishments that would define you as a leader."

Clinton: "People saw me as a leader, as president. They credited me with keeping the economy booming, and not getting into any serious trouble abroad. That means something to people."

Kennedy: "You feel that was enough? To have kept a steady helm? To prevent the boat from rocking?"

Clinton considers. "Okay, yes."

Kennedy: "But how do we effect change – significant change, in health care, education, justice – without rocking the boat?"

Clinton: (shaking his head) "You've got me."

Kennedy: "Do you think it is possible to alter our course, to feed every child, to eliminate violence, without taking serious measures in a different direction? The road less traveled.

Clinton: "I read that book."

Kennedy: "Do you remember from where comes the expression?"

Clinton thinks but shakes his head. "A poet. Ezra Pound?

Kennedy: "Robert Frost. He spoke at my inauguration. The book was by Scott Peck. It was about going your own way. In one of his later books, Peck quoted Mencken as saying, 'The difference between a moral man and a man of honor is that the latter regrets a discreditable act, even when it has worked and he has not been caught.'"

Clinton: (testily) "Are you making a point?"

Kennedy: "Not about you. It was meant as much about where we have been as where we need to go.

Clinton grumbles and is quiet: "So what happens next? Are you supposed to push me overboard?"

Kennedy laughs. "That's not what this was about, Mr. Clinton. It was to talk with The Boy from Hope – that's where you were born, wasn't it?" – (Clinton nods) "to find out how he'd grown."

Clinton: "And you found out?"

Kennedy: "I think so, yes."

Clinton: "Are you surprised?"

Kennedy: "No."

Clinton: "Disappointed?"

Kennedy: "Not really. I didn't have any other expectations. You've presented yourself pretty much the way we saw you in office. Wouldn't you agree that's a fair assessment?"

Clinton ignores the question. "I don't think that you're going to be inviting me to be a member of your group, then?"

Kennedy: "I don't think you'd find it very interesting."

Clinton nods, though he's clearly a little disappointed.

Kennedy turns the wheel and the sail boom shifts from port to starboard above their heads. "I'll take us back to the marina now."

Clinton: "What do I do then?"

Kennedy: "That's up to you. It's always been up to you."

A Tale of One City

Once upon a time, there was a quaint little city by the sea. Founded by artists and other creative types a century earlier, the citizenry was proud of its culture. Size-wise it was tiny but its heart was big so they called it a city.

But dark clouds formed over their city. Unhappy with their last mayor, they elected a good ole boy...or so they thought. Yes, he was a friendly, glad-handing sort of guy who had lived all his life in the city, but there were reports that he treated women disrespect-fully. In fact, the city was forced to investigate to see if there was any truth to the stories, but the nefarious officials limited their inquiry to only his treatment of city employees. The investigation found that while he had not acted in a totally reprehensible manner, he had misbehaved.

Many of the citizens saw the investigation as a white-wash since the mayor had been accused by a number of women who were not city employees of seriously inappropriate behavior, both of a gender intrusion nature and of his financial shenanigans with women renting properties owned by his family. Those allegations, though not formal, wouldn't go away.

There were other reasons why the mayor was under fire. One was that he named his campaign manager to the council seat he vacated to become mayor. Some said that with her personal harshness and regressive politics she never should have been appointed to the council. Some even went to so far as to call her the power behind the throne; that she was influencing the mayor to heighten their political power in the city.

No wonder it was said that a bad smell arose from city hall when the mayor and his appointed councilperson formed a cabal, bringing in a weak-minded council member to produce a majority vote to do their bidding. And their bidding often meant benefitting their friends and causing misery for those out of favor. Indeed, the mayor was so cocky that he reportedly made threats against those who demanded to be treated fairly.

Another move that raised concern was the hiring of the keynote speaker at the mayor's campaign launch to be the city's attorney.

Matters got worse when a reporter claimed that the city attorney had lied on his résumé. The city council met behind closed doors and later reported that they had been shown documents that proved the attorney hadn't lied on his application. The reporter scoffed at the ruse. He sued the city saying they had violated the law by hiding the so-called validating documents from the public.

The controlling members of the city council were so confident – or was it smug? – that rather than waiting a couple of weeks for the court hearing, they went ahead and voted to give the city attorney a five-year, seven-figure contract! The citizenry was outraged, but the cries for tar-'n-feathers were properly mitigated by cooler heads who insisted on waiting for the court hearing.

Only there was another chapter to be written. The scurrilous people plotting the city's future – and their own control of it – came up with a plan to solidify that power. They would get rid of the only person on the council who opposed them...a councilman who stood for transparency, integrity, and decency. Of course, the conspirators weren't going to wait another two years to try to beat him at the polls; they wanted him out now.

Here's how their plan went. The major asked the councilman for a favor: could he find a room for a close friend to stay in town for a couple of nights during an annual special event which had filled all the rooms in all the inns. Alas, the councilman, always seeking to mend fences, agreed to look, and finally offered a room in his own house for only a small fee. The mayor's friend took advantage of the offer, but then refused to pay the councilman, who got bent out of shape by the thievery and made it clear, in no uncertain terms, his view of the tarnished character of the mayor's friend.

Surprise, surprise! The mayor's best friend sued the city for the councilman's rude if understandable expression of ire. What did the council do? They held a special meeting behind closed doors to skewer the councilman for doing a favor for the mayor, though of course that's not the way they put it. Rather, they said, he had put the city at risk of being besmirched and have to pay the claim.

That same week, in the halls of true justice, the distin-guished judge who had the previous Friday heard the case of the closed-door council session that held back the city attorneys' purported substantiation of his questioned credentials...issued his ruling. He denied the city's position in spades, declaring, "The public has a general interest in the 'prevention of secrecy in government.'"

That should have been enough, but the council stalled, announcing that they were consulting with yet an-other attorney on the question of whether or not they should appeal the judge's decision, squandering many thousands of taxpayer dollars in the process. Why would they do that? One popular wag with his finger long on the pulse of city politics had the answer. "It's politics," he said. "The election is in November. They don't want to be voted out of office and they think filing an appeal will save them. But," he added, "that won't work. The people now know they made a mistake – a big mistake – electing their own version of Trump. They think it's time to move on, and quickly."

Nonetheless, the city attorney continued to make sounds like this should go all the way to the Kavanaugh court where he was sure he'd find a kinship verdict. But the council, under pressure from angry citizens, said they'd release the documents within 15 days of the judge issuing his written decision...which could mean the documents would come to light two weeks before the election. The incumbents on the ballot couldn't be happy about this, because the documents would show that they either hired a city attorney who perhaps wasn't quite truthful with them, or they spent all that money going to court trying to hide something that didn't need hiding in the first place.

For a while, speculation of all sorts blew through the town like a northern version of the Santa Ana's. Would the set-up councilman ask Robert Mueller to go after the miscreants on charges of illicit collusion? And had the nefarious councilwoman dispatched her faithful lapdog (the mayor) and the city's pettifogger (the city attorney) to find some eye of newt and toe of frog, wool of bat and tongue of dog?

Um, no, and all (or most) of the rumors dried up the night of the election. That was when twenty minutes after the polls closed, it became clear that the incumbent dog and his lap were out on their ears. And by a huge margin. Ultimately the city attorney got one thing right: he resigned.

Spring of 1968

This essay was accepted for publication in the Exeter alumni magazine in 2018, my 50th reunion year.

I have a different account of what happened in 1968, the year of my graduation.

I'd arrived as a Lower Middler in September of 1965. That first year was a challenge. My parents received a letter from the school the following July recommending that they consider withdrawing me. I informed my parents that I was returning to Exeter, where I got myself sufficiently together during my Upper Middler year.

My senior year was amazing, particularly that last five months. It was very political and confirmed my path in life, both as a journalist and a political maven.

In February of 1968, George Romney, then governor of Michigan and candidate for the Republican presidential nomination, came to speak at Exeter. Romney had recently returned from a "fact-finding" trip to Vietnam, after which he said he'd been "brainwashed" into supporting the war.

As he walked out of the gym where he'd given his speech, I sidled up next to him and asked, "Governor, are you still brainwashed?" He reached over, tousled my hair and turning to formal members of the press, offered with a chuckle, "Next question."

On March 1st Allard Lowenstein, who was a primary organizer of the McCarthy for President campaign, arrived in Exeter. I met with him for an hour in The Grill and we strategized about mounting a local campaign for the Minnesota senator in Exeter and the surrounding area.

We had twelve days before the New Hampshire primary. Two days later a student organizational meeting was held in the Academy Building. Dozens of people got involved, along with a number of faculty members including George Mellor and Chuck Trout. Working in conjunction with McCarthy people who'd opened a storefront on Water Street, we blanketed the area, knocking hundreds of doors, talking up McCarthy's candidacy.

(I remember walking down Front Street toward the storefront carrying a McCarthy for President sign when a local stuck his head out the window of his car and yelled, "Stupid kid, Tail Gunner Joe died ten years ago."

Another visitor to Exeter in March was Richard Nixon.

He held a press conference in the basement of Kurtz's restaurant. On a sheet of paper, I had typed "This is to attest that Anthony M. Seton is an editorial representative of Inquest Publications." It got me into the press conference. Nixon went around the small gathering of news people, and when he came to me, I told him that I had cleaned his daughter, Julie's, room when I was on the building and grounds crew at Smith College the summer before, and that I'd been a goalie on David Eisenhower's soccer team. David and Julie were an item by then.

I thought that would endear me enough to the presidential candidate to call on me for a question, which was, "You say you will boost funds for the military fighting in Vietnam and fix our inner cities. How can you do that and cut taxes?" But although Nixon shared our interchange with the room, he didn't call on me for a question. (Sigh)

Gene McCarthy lost New Hampshire to Lyndon Johnson by only seven points, 42% to 49%, an incredible upset that – along with Robert Kennedy entering the race – forced the incumbent president out of the race less than three weeks later. (A couple of carloads of Exonians were driven down to Marblehead, Massachusetts for a couple of Saturdays to campaign for McCarthy in April. He beat Kennedy, whose late entry into the race meant he hadn't gotten organized, 49% to 28%.)

After the McCarthy campaign, Chuck and Margot

Trout organized students to canvas the area to garner signatures in support of the Fair Housing Act that was before Congress. On April 4th, by a slim margin, the Senate passed the measure. That evening Martin Luther King, Jr. was assassinated. The House passed, and President Johnson signed, this important civil rights legislation into law a week later.

That spring, the Vietnam War was heating up to its lethal worst for American troops, and the nation was on edge. I organized a two-day weekend conference on Vietnam for students from six schools. It included speakers, discussions, and films held in the Lamont Gallery. On that Sunday, attention turned to campus protests with unplanned (but welcomed) discussions presented by two Exeter seniors who had just returned from the demonstrations at Columbia University.

The last week of school was the first week in June, and I was given special permission by the Hoyt Hall dorm master, Leroy Willoughby, to stay up late and watch the California primary returns in the common room. Shortly before midnight, seeing that McCarthy would lose, I went to bed before the results were announced. The next morning, my roommate, Vince Robertson, came back to our rooms from breakfast and asked if I knew what happened. I told him, "Yeah, McCarthy lost." That's when he told me that Robert Kennedy had been shot.

Kennedy died on June 6th. Three days later, on the lawn in front of the Academy Building, the class of

1968 listened politely to Dean Acheson, grandfather of our classmate, David, speak in the present tense of an era that was on its way out. Then Richard W. Day, Exeter's 10th principal, called us up individually by name, and handed us our diplomas.

I went on to become a television news producer for ABC where I covered Watergate, six elections, and five space shots. I produced Barbara Walters new interviews and earned a handful of national awards for producing business/economics coverage. I continued my journalist endeavors over the years and taught journalism at the college and graduate level. I also got into politics, consulting on campaigns for Tom Campbell, Nancy Pelosi, the American Nurses Association, and a score of local races in California.

And it continues today. Thank you, Exeter.

The Young Man and the Sea

It was more than 50 years ago that Bert Cutino and his partner, Ted Balestreri, opened the Sardine Factory in Monterey. Still thriving, the restaurant sits two blocks above Cannery Row where for decades Bert's family used to sell the fish they pulled out of Monterey Bay and the Pacific Ocean. His forebears were among a thousand emigrant fishermen from a small port town in Sicily at the beginning of the last century. The fathers took up fishing here while the mothers worked in the canneries.

Bert was brought up on Spaghetti Hill – some call it Garlic Hill – in Monterey, and described his early life as being brought up around food. He noted that, "Growing up in a Sicilian family or Italian family, food always is the centerpiece of the whole family." His mother was considered one of the best cooks in the area, and he remembers helping her out with the food from the time he was five years old, rolling the dough for the *cucidati*, Christmas cookies made with figs.

Bert didn't plan to go into the food industry. Rather he

was attracted to teaching. He loved learning "about different countries, cultures, and how a lot of things came into existence." But life is what happens to the plans we make. The summer Bert was 13, his older brother Pete got him a dish washing summer job at the Holman's Guest Ranch in Carmel Valley. One day the resort chef fed the staff spaghetti. Bert didn't take any and when the chef asked why, Bert replied, "Chef, I'm Italian."

Eyebrows raised at the youngster, the chef asked could Bert make it better.

"Yeah," was the boy's simple answer.

The chef told him the next time Bert would make it. And he did, the way his mother made tomato sauce, the way it's made in the Sardine Factory today. The key extra ingredient was sugar which cut the acid of the tomatoes. The resort owner, Mr. Holman, came by later in the day, tasted Bert's dish, and promptly ordered the chef to serve it to the customers, not the staff.

Though he didn't know it at the time, Bert was on his way to culinary greatness, but first he did a brief stint working on his father's fishing boat, the 38-footer *Santa Rosalia*. This was 1953, and a time of significant change in the local fishing industry. There was still a wide variety of fish to be caught, including pompano, kingfish, sea bass, halibut, salmon, and even some 30-plus-foot whale sharks. ("We towed it in, 'cause you can't put it on the boat, and they give you $25 bucks for a shark in those days.") Plus there were scallops, mussels, crabs, and calamari to be harvested, but there were no sardines. The once thriving sardine industry had collapsed in the 40s.

When the sardines were gone, the fishing industry was hard hit. The owners of the big boats especially. They were fitted with huge purse seine nets that would stretch out for a mile or more and be pulled through the water for a day or two, hauling in large schools of the fish. But such fishing didn't work when the sardines disappeared because the larger fish that were left didn't swim in dense schools. Some of the big boats had cost $150,000 in the 1930s and were now useless. Some of them wound up being sold for as little as $10,000, for scrap or to fishermen in other parts of the world's oceans. (This historical note: Bert's uncle, who had a 90-foot boat, the *US Liberator*, was a friend of John Steinbeck.)

Things would be all right for the owners of the smaller boats, like the *Santa Rosalia*, but Bert's father was not optimistic. He made a statement that the boy never forgot. "He said enjoy the fish that we're getting now because by the time you reached my age you will not see it anymore. He said we bring in the fish to the market and the market doesn't tell us what they really want until we get to the dock. And then when we get there, because we catch as much as we can, we have to throw a lot overboard."

Bert recalled the boats lined up at the market in Monterey, one boat after another. They all had made catches by putting out their gill nets for a day or two. Then they started pulling in the nets on their way to the docks. Their nets stretched out a maybe mile, and it would take three or four hours while bobbing up and down in the waves bringing all the net in, only then seeing what they'd caught, hoping there would be a market for it.

Of course, what the markets wouldn't pay for was thrown over the side; there was a limited market in those days because people weren't eating fish. Or they were eating frozen products like fish sticks. But then people started becoming health conscious, and fresh fish was big on the menu. As the demand grew, little by little, fish species started to disappear. As Bert's father had said, the ocean could only produce so much.

"That was almost 70 years ago," Bert recalled. "I was really amazed that my father and a lot of these old-time fishermen were really environmentalists in so many ways. They really wanted to preserve the fish."

Today, the fishermen and the markets are guided by a number of organizations that define sustainable limits for various denizens of the sea. Here on the California Central Coast, the Monterey Bay Aquarium has been a leader in determining which species are in danger of being over-fished. But they are not alone in the process, and it is often a challenge to determine which species and sub-species need protection.

For the restaurants, it also matters where the fish are caught. Bert noted that he had people walking out of his restaurant because the Aquarium said that sword-fish should not be served. But the Aquarium wasn't distinguishing between the swordfish caught on the East coast, where the supply was greater, and the local swordfish that needed to be protected. Bert has strong-ly encouraged the Aquarium to be more specific about which fish truly needed protection.

Another environmental issue that has come to the fore is pollution. Pollution – both the chemicals and the trash, and particularly plastics – is a disaster for the oceans. What's being found in the bellies of the fish is frightening. The chemical pollution is not only danger-ous for the fish, but also for those who eat the fish. You may recall the exposé about mercury in tuna fish fifty years ago.

Regrettably, little has been done to protect the sea life from the wanton disrespect by those dumping garbage and chemicals, both into the waterways that feed into the oceans and into the oceans themselves. The fact is that pollution threatens an irreplaceable source of nutrition. Dead zones from pollution are popping up around the world.

Another serious problem has developed from the rising temperatures due to climate change, which has resulted in the dislocation and disruption in the natural breeding patters of large numbers of sea life. This has affected not only the fish, but the fishing industry and the food supply.

Another aspect of the climate change and pollution crises is lower levels of oxygen in the water. I had sent to Bert a *New York Times* article by Kendra Pierre-Louis ("Waters Off California Acidifying Faster Than Rest of Oceans, Study Shows") and ran into him a week later at a luncheon where he railed against what is happening in Monterey Bay. He said that people don't understand that oxygen in the sea is vital to the life of the fish, just as it is to humans and animals on land. He has been clamoring about the acidification and the lowering of oxygen levels for five years, urging the national and international restaurant and chef organizations to get more involved, before it's too late.

"We're going to where there will just be farm fish someday," Bert said. "Good, bad or indifferent, there will be no more wild fish. And we all know that fish living in the wild have a whole different flavor and texture than the farm raised fish." One might suppose that consumers will ultimate be resigned to the lesser qualities, but it's shameful to think that we are failing to prevent this eventuality.

"I believe it is a climate change situation. I think it's a big problem, even though maybe the president doesn't want to face it and other people don't want to face the realities of it. We've got to get back to the realities of the situation. We've got to figure away how are we going to keep that oxygen flowing in this ocean.

"I've experienced climate change; right here at Monterey and the ocean I saw the difference. Abalone used to live 30, 40, 50 years and grow to 12 to 14 inches. Today they're three, four, five inches. The Dungeness crab, oysters, clams...they're showing chemical contamination. You can't trust the wild oysters. And even though the flavor is not the same, you get the farm oysters. And even that you've got to worry about."

Bert remembered his youth on his father's boat. "When I saw the fish being thrown away, it just broke my heart. We caught this fish for nothing. My father said, 'What am I going to do? This is my livelihood. This is what I do. We're at the mercy of the markets. We're at the mercy of the canneries.'" Today the situation is more dire. The global population in 1953 was 2.6 billion. Today we're at 7.7 billion. Where do we find the food for all these people? Where do we put their waste?

Now Bert is pushing the major restaurant and culinary associations to take an active role in protecting and restoring the environment. He is also struggling with what he sees as over-zealousness or misdirection, such as efforts to end cooking with natural gas. For instance, he's strongly opposed to a new ordinance in the city of Berkeley which bans natural gas in new buildings. "Cooking on electric stoves...I cannot cook on electric stoves. I cook with gas because I under-stand how it works. How it heats the pan. How it flows." Any serious cook will agree. Surely, he says, there are more significant ways to fight global warm-ing.

Throughout his years as one of the most recognized and successful chefs in the world, Bert Cutino has received over a hundred national and international culinary awards. But since he was a boy wanting to be a teacher, his principal interest has always been education – his own and that of others. Much of his life has been spent learning from top chefs like Paul Prudhomme and contributing his experience-born knowledge at seminars and through the media.

Several decades ago, when then-Assemblyman (and later Congressman) Sam Farr of Monterey asked for his help on a non-political issue, Bert jokingly retorted, "What's in it for Hospitality?" Not long thereafter, the legislature passed a measure submitted by Farr with funds supporting California culinary colleges.

What the Ball Didn't Say

His arm felt as heavy as a side of beef. He had pitched 26 outs to the bottom of the ninth inning, and it was only a last drop of resolve that kept him from breaking into screams and tears. He'd faced 28 batters and tossed 87 pitches. There had been errors by two of his infielders that allowed men on base but neither had reached second. He started feeling the strain of what he might accomplish after the seventh inning, and it had taken considerable effort to focus on throwing the ball rather than thinking about pitching his name into the history books. That extra focus had added to the physical fatigue. He'd pitched full games before; he'd certainly thrown more pitches. But he'd never been in the position he was in now, perhaps a single pitch way from a no-hitter. And his right arm felt like lead...lead that throbbed with the threat that it could come off with the ball if he weren't careful.

The whole stadium was abuzz, naturally, but it wasn't his care. Nor were the seven men around him, nor even the man behind the plate. His catcher had done a great job - a perfect job so far - of calling the pitches. The pitcher laughed to himself when the thought crossed his mind that it was up to him to put the ball past the batter, rather than let him get a bat on it which would put the game in someone else's hands.

So far he'd dispatched this batter three times, but two of the balls had nearly found their way to the hits column. He had been tough on the pitcher all year, getting on base half the times he'd faced him. Yes, the pitcher could grind him and put his faith in his fielders, but the man with the bat had the power to reach the fences, and even if he only got a hit, there would go his best game. The bottom line was that the man on the mound knew that he had only one pitch left in him.

Suddenly a smile came to him which he quickly hid from his lips. He jerked his head down to look at the glove on his left hand. Then he lifted it to his left ear and listened to it for several seconds. He took the ball out of the glove and put the glove under his left arm. With both hands he turned the ball over and over, holding it in front of eyes, peering at it. Then he looked over the ball at the batter. He nodded his head slowly and thoughtfully.

He put his glove back on, slipped the ball into the glove, and got ready to throw, placing his right foot in its place by the rubber. He looked toward the catcher who looked back inscrutably from behind his mask. The catcher gave him a series of meaningless signs except for the one that called for a fastball. The pitcher nodded, though he knew he didn't have enough arm left to make it very fast.

He pumped, and pumped again, not something he'd ever done before. Then he reared back and with all the pretense he could managed, he pegged the ball toward the plate. He was aiming for a spot on the inside corner, maybe six inches above the batter's waist because the man liked the ball best when it was low and outside.

That late in the game, it normally would have been difficult for the ball to find its way to where the pitcher wanted it to go because normally the pitcher would have been using his last bit of strength to put oomph on the ball. But this wasn't normal. The "fast-ball" reached the plate traveling at only eighty miles an hour, considerably slower than the pitcher had been throwing during the game.

The poor batter had had extra time to try to figure out what the pitcher would throw at him, but he had limited his guesses to only two. With a one-and-two count, it would have been normal - again that word - for the pitcher to waste a pitch, giving him something high and outside. But the batter had been watching the pitcher and knew he was tired. How tired, it was impossible to know. Did he have enough for one last heater, to try and blow the ball across the plate for the third strike? Those were the choices as the batter saw it, and the longer he had to think, the more wound up he got.

When a good batter thinks too much, he draws power from his instinct, and inevitably his inclination is to lash out. What is he going to lash out against? Why the ball, of course, and with extra speed and power.

Compounding the batter's sense of urgency was the double-pump and the mountain of energy that seemed to form behind the pitch. So when the ball finally headed his way, the batter began to uncoil. It took only a fraction of a second for a synapse in of his brain to recognize that something was wrong, and emergency instructions were sent through his chest, shoulders, arms, and hands to hold back. But when you have invested yourself into smashing a small white orb flying at you at 95 miles an hour, or so you expect, it's hard to put the brakes on all that energy. And it requires almost an impossible amount of precision to redirect that force such that any of the bat - let alone the desired sweet spot - will then scribe an arc that will have it meet the ball squarely on its path across the plate.

It was really too much to ask. The arms were planning its assault with the bat according to a critical velocity factor that the ball simply didn't have. Giving the batter credit, he did manage to cut the power behind his swing, but he lacked the coordination to also reset the location where the meat part of the bat and the ball would intersect. The batter was thinking that the ball would be where he wanted it, low and outside, but the pitcher, knowing this would be his last pitch and knowing he didn't have to overpower the batter this time, used precision instead of power and placed it high and inside.

Only after several stop-action replays did it seem to show that the bat actually touched the ball, but it was certainly not with enough force to deflect it. The catcher had watched the ball virtually float in and when the ball flew by the bat, his glove was there waiting with its fat leather smile to capture it. He squeezed the ball with his glove as his other hand covered it tightly.

The umpire jerked his hand up to call the third strike, and the stadium erupted. The catcher ran out to the mound where he joined the rest of the team, first in mobbing the pitcher and then lifting him to their shoulders before carrying him to the dugout. The mayhem continued into the locker room where the pitcher was soon surrounded by media types all asking the typically unbrilliant questions like "How does it feel?"

The pitcher had seen *Bull Durham* and had learned much from what Kevin Costner had explained to Tim Robbins. He was golly-gee-whiz in awe of what happened and couldn't have done it without God and his teammates, his mom, and apple pie. When report-ers asked him what he had heard from the ball, mean-ing when he had held it in his glove next to his ear, he answered "Nothing" with a blank face and went back to other questions. Finally, he pleaded for his right to take a shower and he escaped.

For the time being. When he got to his Mustang convertible in the player's lot an hour later, he was surprised to find a cute young thang representing a local underground paper. She stood with her butt against the driver's side door. "So when you said you heard 'nothing' from the ball, what was it that you thought you'd heard?"

The pitcher had his second moment of brilliance that day, probably an occurrence as unusual as pitching a (near) perfect game. He said he didn't know. The reporter didn't move. The pitcher seemed to relent. He asked her if she would accept the truth if he told her off the record. That surprised her but she nodded. He looked at her recording device which she had been holding up to him and now switched it off.

He looked around to make sure there was no one in hearing distance. Then he leaned closer to the reporter and said, "I asked the ball what I should do to get it by the bat."

The reporter was startled, less by what he said than by his candor. She managed to ask, "And?"

The pitcher shrugged. "I told you, it didn't say anything." Then with his hand, he waved her out of the way of his car. Somewhat stunned, she complied. He got into his car, closed the door, and started the car.

The reporter recovered her senses. "Do you do that a lot?"

The pitcher shook his head vigorously. "No. Only when I'm pitching a no-hitter." With that he put the car into gear and drove off.

It Is Never about Luck

This is a piece from my novel, *Deki-san*. Cody Howard is a former network news correspondent who finds himself in a downward professional spiral. He moves into a house next to Roy Deki. It turns out that it wasn't by any means a coincidence. On several occasion, in various ways, Deki-san provides Cody with invaluable perspective. And then saves his life.

"It is never about luck," said Deki. "Luck is a word invented to explain what people don't understand. It may be that the universe is perceived as chaotic, but that is because its order doesn't fit into the understanding of lower human reason. It is why when some tragic event occurs to children or other innocents, religious people wrap themselves in the thin cloak of 'It's God's will.'"

"I can appreciate the idea that there is no such thing as luck," Cody replied. "It's just what happens. But as far as people explaining away indefensible events as

'God's will,' surely that's little different from saying the universe is orderly."

"It's entirely different. One is seeking explanations. The other isn't. There is always a series of circumstances that leads to a moment in time, to an event. That's the only explanation there is. There is no reasoning to why this child was molested by a priest or that family died in a car wreck. Just facts that preceded the events. It is like people who need to imbue a shark with the purpose to murder. The shark is eating to survive. It is the most primitive instinct. There is no morality involved. There is no murderous intent."

Cody was silent for a long moment as he digested the man's ideas. "And we anthropomorphize the shark, giving it human emotions, for what purpose?"

Deki smiled. "To provide a target object for their fear. Civilization is at a stage of living life in conflict. There is the presumption of struggle. It is part of our language; for instance, we have to *earn* a living. But even for the wealthy, they create problems in their life that they have to face. The dressmaker won't have the $50,000 gown ready for the charity ball. The private jet couldn't get clearance because of bad weather. The accountant could only write off half of the vacation. Conflict is what defines us, whether it is real or manufactured."

The Twain Gang

This is the third in the series of *From the Garden of Continuing Reflection*. It was originally written in January 2002. I had just re-read *Adventures of Huck Finn* and *The Adventures of Tom Sawyer*, and rued, not for the first time, how much great literature that was assigned in school was viewed as a burden rather than experienced with joy. Also, young minds often lack the frame of reference to appreciate the importance – historical and literary – of such works as those two (among others) by Mark Twain, as well as by many other great authors.

I need to say of *Huck Finn* and *Tom Sawyer* that in my more recent perusal of these two extraordinary books, I felt as though I was reading them for the first time. But that was a dozen years ago, and in re-reading this piece, I am reminded, both of the value of Twain's stories and how I've forgotten many of the references to them in the piece below.

* * * * *

By the way, apropos of nothing, did you know that Mark Twain was born, and died, under Halley's Comet?

Also, did you know that *The Adventures of Huckleberry Finn* was first published in the United Kingdom in 1884 and in the United States in 1885?

* * * * *

MARK TWAIN walks through the front door of a restaurant called Jus Jim's, wearing his trademark white suit. He looks around and sees HUCKLEBERRY FINN seated at a table in the corner. Huck is wearing a button-down shirt under a worn but quality tweed sports jacket with a pair of neat jeans. Twain walks over to the table. Huck stands. They shake hands and sit down.

Twain: You look great, Huck. The years haven't painted a line on you.

Huck: Why thank ya, Mr. Twain. (pauses; belying his truth) Ya look purdy much the same as ye did back then.

Twain: Maybe a little more careworn. It's been more of a struggle than maybe it should have been.

Huck: (looks sympathetic) I heard ya lost a daughter and yer wife. Real sorry 'bout that.

Twain: Thanks. It was a long time ago, but it doesn't go away. (forces a smile) So how have you been? I haven't seen you since I finished your book, more than a century ago.

Huck: (smiles) My book?

Twain: Yes, *Adventures of Huckleberry Finn*.

Huck: That's what the title says, but I'm not sure it was really my book.

Twain: (surprised) Huck, what are you saying?

Huck: Oh, t'was a great book, make no mind 'bout that.

Twain: But?

Huck: I jus' wonder'd if maybe ya got done with it but didn't know the endin'. No offense, Mr. Twain.

Twain: I recall you saying something like that when I finished the first draft. I didn't understand what you said then and I don't now. You didn't like the ending?

Huck: (shrugs) It seemed kinda 'brupt.

Twain: (eyes narrow) Is that it? Or is that you didn't like my putting Tom back in as a main character?

A nerve's been struck, though Huck tries to mask it. He is aided in his deception when he looks up to see

TOM SAWYER approaching. Tom is dressed in a nice but not ostentatious suit, and is walking with a notice-able limp. Huck stands to greet his old friend. Twain turns around and sees Tom, and he stands as well. There are hello's all around and hand-shaking and hugs and back-slapping. They regain their seats.

Tom: Well, ain't this grand! What a good idea, Huck? Mr. Twain, you don't look a day older than the last time we were all together.

Twain: We've got a lot to catch up on. (He eyes Huck, silently agreeing to let the earlier subject drop, for the time being.)

Tom: And Huckleberry Finn, you look as fancy-free in spirit as ever. You must have loved the beatnik and hippie years.

Huck: (laughs) Never saw no dif'rence.

They laugh.

JIM walks up to the table. He is wearing a large white chef's hat.

Jim: Gemmin, how good to sees y'all 'gin.

They three rise and Tom and Huck exchange hugs with Jim. Twain is more reserved and just shakes hands. Jim tells them to sit down.

Jim: I jus' want'd to give ya mah personal welcome. (gestures to the rest of the diners) Can't stay. Got a rest'rant full o' people 'gin tonight. Gotta cook for 'em.

Huck: 'T's this way every night. Jim jus' got writ up as one of the top five restaurant in The Big Easy. (turns to his friend) Fourth year in row, Jim?

Jim: Das right, Mars Huck.

Tom: (looks at the two) So you fellas have been in touch over the years?

Jim looks to Huck.

Huck: Uh, I looked Jim up 'bout five years back.

Jim: Tell 'em, Mars Huck. Tell 'em what you done for ole Jim.

Huck: (smiles at Jim) I was surfin' the net lookin' for places to eat when I was comin' to N' Orleans. 'N I saw a photograph of a place where Jim was workin' as the real chef behind some big sports c'lebrity who actual owned the restaurant.

Jim: (excited) So when he come to town, he looks me up at da udder place. I near as turned white when I see'd him. So he has dinner 'n waits for me 'n when I'se done, we go foh a walk down by da river and we talks. Til the sun come up. (He looks to Huck who nods.) 'N den he aks me why ah don' have mah own place, what I be doin' all da cookin' n' all. 'N I laughs and says, Mars Huck, da white men still have da cash. (beams at Huck) So he jus'...

Huck: So I said, Jim, what if I cud find the cash, would ya know how to run it, 'cause I don't know nothin' 'bout how restaurant works. And turns out, his wife was a-runnin' the business side of the place where Jim was workin'.

Jim: Mars Huck helped us with the financin' an: we open'd rights here five years ago las month.

Tom: That's great, Jim. A damn site better than Phelps jail.

They all laugh with him.

Jim: I'll catch ya all after you'se eats. 'N it's on me, whatever ya alls wan'.

They protest.

Jim: (holds up his hands to stop them) No way you'se going reach in yoh pock't at ole Jim's. Not t'night, not ever. Ya all gave me what I have today. Leas' I cud do.

They thank him. Jim walks away.

Tom: Who'd a thunk? Twaren't so many miles up the river that Jim was a slave.

Huck: Who 'mos got hung...

Tom: ...Til we evaded him from his cell.

Twain: (to Tom) I saw you limping when you came in. That a result of your taking a bullet in the leg during the escape?

Tom: (raps his knuckles on his leg, making a hollow sound) Yessir. It wound up getting infected. They had to take it just above the knee.

Twain: I'm sorry. I didn't mean for it to be so serious.

Tom: (waves him off) No need to apologize. I think it was my punishment for keeping Jim in jail when he could have gone free the day I arrived. (smiles) Still, it was quite an adventure.

Huck: (looking thoughtful) 'Deed it was that, Tom Sawyer.

Twain: So what have you boys been doing since '85?

They look at each other, Tom with his palms up, Huck pointing to Tom .

Tom: I guess I'll go first. Well, first and foremost, I got married. Becky, of course. Somethin' about the time we spent in the cave, not thinkin' we'd ever get out, kinda set things for us. Best thing that ever happened to me, that gal. She and the gimp leg (raps on the knee again) helped me settle down a little, at least on the outside. Judge Thatcher came to me before we got hitched and said he would take care of getting me through college and law school if I would promise to take care of his daughter right, but it wasn't no problem for me, 'cause like I said, back in the cave...that sealed things for Becky and me.

A WAITER comes to the table and when Tom finishes speaking and looks up.

Waiter: Jim would like to select your dishes, gentlemen, if that's all right.

Tom: Just so long there's no rope ladder in my food.

Twain and Huck laugh and the waiter smiles indulgently.

Tom: (for the others) That will be fine, thank you. (The Waiter departs) So I went to law school, passed the Missouri bar the first shot, and the old Judge – he was really a smart fellow – he said maybe we needed to get away from St. Petersburg and he arranged for me to join a practice in Jefferson City. Mostly contracts and stuff; no criminal. A few years later, our local state legislator broke his neck climbing out the back window of somebody else's house, and because of my own notoriety, they appointed me to fill out his term. Then I won in the next election, and served three terms altogether. Nothing much exciting to speak of, makin' laws and spendin' the taxpayers' money, what little there was of it, and never enough to do anything right. About that time, our son Langhorne – we named him after you, Mr. Twain (a smile appears on Twain's face) – was getting to where he needed a father to help shape him, so I went back to my law practice where there was less traveling and I could spend more time with him, and our daughter, Martha.

Twain: You've done well for yourself, my boy.

Tom: It's been a passable life, sure. Not too exciting, but exciting enough. Probably would have been different if I'd had two good legs, but I don't have any regrets. (turns) What about you, Huckleberry?

Huck: (looks down at the table; contemplates; looks up) Not so sedentary as you, Tom . Did a lot of travel-in'.

Tom (smiling) Hardly surprising.

Huck: First I went west to California fer a few years, then north to Alaska but it was too cold, so I jumped a tramp steamer 'n worked my way down to Japan. I stayed in the Ori'nt, goin' from port to port, stayin' here a few days 'n there some. Musta been a good ten years o' driftin' with the tide, you might say. 'N then I thought to see Europe. Tom , you never know'd the king 'n the duke, but I was jus' a might curious about what they were talkin', even if they jus' got it from books, mos'ly the Duke Bilgewater.

So I got passage to Marseilles, 'n afterwards walk'd mos' the way 'cross France, slow-like, gettin' the local flavor. I saw Paris, 'n then headed up to the Low Countries. Didn't wanna go to Germany; heard bad things about that country. 'Sted, I crost The Channel to England. Spent lot o' time in Scotland. Liked those folks. Always ready to sit down 'n have a pipe with a stranger. Then I d'cided maybe I should come home, which I did. Never cud settle anywhere. I got a small place up the Mendocino coast, California that I think of as my home, but mostly I'm on the road, seein' new vistas.

Twain: You seem happy enough with your life, Huck.

Huck: Truly I am, Mr. Twain. I knows it looks like I'm los' or somethin', but fact is, I'm not lookin' for anything. Mostly, I jus' like floatin' past it. I don't bother the world, and it lets me go on my own way, wherever that is.

The Waiter returns and announces the dishes as he puts them down in front of the men.

Waiter: We have Jim's catfish cakes, Jim's skewered shrimps, Jim's pork balls. (He displays each of the dishes and doles out portions to each of the diners and departs. They begin eating, and obviously enjoying the food; lots of oohs and aahs.)

Twain: I guess we won't have much trouble remembering the name of this place.

Huck: (chuckles) Funny you should say that. (chuckles again) Back when Jim was openin' this place, he was so 'xcited 'n grateful. (interrupts himself; to Twain) Did you know that our frien' here (gestures to Tom) give Jim the money to buy his wife 'n chilluns outta slavery.

Twain: Good for you, Tom. Though I'm not surprised.

Tom smiles modestly

Huck: Anyway, so Jim's so 'cited 'bout the rest'rant, givin' back, and embracin' the spirit of his life what we give him that he says he's gonna call this place Niggah

Jim's.

Twain: Oh my.

Huck: He was 'fraid people wouldn' know which Jim he was. Not the baseball pitcher sellin' drawers or some football Jim sellin' somethin' else.

Tom: (laughs) You talked him out of it, I see?

Huck: I 'xplain'd to him 'bout political correct'dness and how that name might upset some folks, 'specially some who got money and wud be customers. "No need upset no one before we'se open," Jim said, and he called the place Jus Jim's.

Tom: But he kept the patois.

Huck: (nods) Said he needed to "keep some 'v dat 'storical ac'racy." He sez his patrons love it, even though some of them think they shouldn't. You know how white folks is, he says.

Tom: (licks his lips appreciatively) Delicious. By the way, how'd you manage the financing, if I may ask? Did you get rich along the way?

Huck: (laughs) I did, ya know, jus' on that six thousand we pulled outta the cave. The Judge, he invested it fer me. Said he hitched a caboose to some train somehow, and it brought in a lotta money. I never touch'd it, because I jus' lived on what I made here 'n there doin' odd jobs, sailin' and fishin' n' stuff. 'N fact, there was plenty there when ole Jim said he be ready to go out on his own. Funny thing is, I didn't even use mah own money, no sir. (He paused for effect) It was really Jim's own money that we used; I jus' made 'rangements so he cud use it fer his restaurant here.

Twain: (looking around) Where did Jim get that kind of money?

Huck: (chuckles; to Tom) Remember how Jim tol' Uncle Silas and Mr. Burton about the duke and the king, 'n what they got caught 'n tar'd n' feather'd n' run outta town on a rail? (Tom nods) Well turns out there was a reward on both them villains. A considerable amount on the duke 'cause he'd tricked some widow womans up in Illinois, left 'em poh. 'N 'cause it turned out that Jim was a free man, they give him the money. 'Bout five thousand, I remember. 'Course Jim didn't know what to do with that kinda money, 'n since it didn't come to him until maybe a year later, when he already got out his family, he giv'd me the money 'n tol' me to 'vest it fer him. Shucks, I jus' give it to the Judge n' tol' him to do the same with it as mine. 'Fore ya know it, Jim's got plen'y o' money he doesn't know what to do with, but he says to me, 'Mars Huck, don' tell me how much is I got 'n don' give me none o' it unless I need it.' He's ac'uly a wealthy man.

Twain: Not bad for a slave.

Tom: He can't buy back those years without his family, but he seems to be makin' a far stab at it.

The waiter clears away the plates.

Twain: Say Tom, before you arrived, Huck was saying that he thought the ending of his story was kinda – he used the word "abrupt". I got the feeling that he thought you had too much of a role in his story.

Tom: (sits back and looks back and forth at the other two) I thought there was somethin' going on when I arrived. (laughs) Truth is, Mr. Twain, I did kinda feel like I might have been hornin' in on Huck's game. He was doin' quite well without me. In fact, I kinda mucked things up.

Twain: It would have been 'nuf for you just to show up, tell Huck that Jim was free and y'all go home?

Tom: (shrugs; wry smile) Huck probably thinks so. And I know Jim could have done without the snakes and spiders and rats.

Huck: (nods) 'N we wud'na drove Aunt Sally near 'round the bend, stealing her spoons 'n candles 'n clothes off the line.

Twain: (laughs) Everybody's a critic. With all due humility, boys, my book is considered one of the great classics of American literature. (clears his throat) Now some might now say that's a very deep pool, and so be it, I'm still floatin'.

They all laugh.

Huck: Now Mr. Twain, see here, I'm not raggin' on

yer writin', sure not. I mean, where would I be if it weren' fer you. I'm right 'preciative o' everythin' you give me. Even killin' pap, you did right by me.

Twain: But...?

Huck: I just kinda think maybe we'd a had plenty of adventures by then.

Twain: True enough. But Huck, I had to get word down to the Phelps' that Jim had been given his freedom. If not, you would have broken him out and never have known that he was a free man. He never would have gotten his family back.

Tom: (interjects) Or learned to cook such fine food.

Twain: And Tom was on his way – that's why you were welcomed so warmly.

Huck: I followed that part.

Twain: Well, Huck, I couldn't just have Tom show up with the news. Such a powerful character doesn't just suddenly become an errand boy. Besides, I needed for you to be in on the conclusion. It was the town that took care of the king and the duke.

Huck: (thinks about it) Okay, I sorta see that part.

Tom: And besides, if I may, Mr. Twain...

Twain: Go right ahead.

Tom: Well, Huck, in that last part, you showed how

you would stand up to me. You showed your independence. Coming of age, I think they call it in the literary world.

Huck: (a little rueful; allows himself to brighten) I guess I can see that, too.

Twain: I hadn't thought about it in quite those terms, Tom , but you're certainly right. (chuckles) You know it's funny how people can figure out stuff the writer himself didn't know.

Tom: Oh, I think you knew it, maybe not consciously, but you must have known it 'cause that's what you wrote.

Twain: Huck?

Huck: Yeah?

Twain: Would you have preferred a different ending? Did you have something in mind?

Tom: Of course he did. He wanted to go back up river and find Mary Jane Wilks.

Huck: (flustered; reddens) I, I sure, um, well, I wudda liked to know that she gotten her slaves back. And maybe did they go to England with the real uncles...'n, 'n stuff.

Twain: I didn't realize you had such a crush on Mary Jane.

Huck: Nah, warn' like that. Warn' no crush. It's jus'

that she was a true righteous girl, and I felt bad lettin' the king sell her slaves out from un'r 'neath her.

Tom: I think it was more coming of age, Huck. Mr. Twain was showin' that you were growing up and having manly urges.

Huck: Aw, come on, now. T'warn' none of that kinda stuff in my book.

Tom: Huck, boy, you weren't payin' attention. The Hairlip sure was makin' a play for you.

Huck: What are you talkin'?

Tom: Did you think she was just being polite to you?

Huck: She didn't trus' me. She was tryin' to get me to make a slip. (thinks back) Which I did.

Tom: I would have taken it as flirting.

Huck: Maybe you wud'na iffn you'da been there 'sted of jus' readin' the book.

Waiter (arrives with an assistant and starts placing dishes on the table, announcing as he goes along) Jim's braised flank steak, Jim's sauteed abalone, Jim's oriental minced pigeon, Jim's chicken-fried gator – it tastes a lot like Jim's chicken fried steak – plus Jim's garlic okra, Jim's oven-baked beans, Jim's cheese potatoes, and Jim's tomatoes stuffed with tabouli and parsley.

Tom: (thanking the Waiter) That looks like it should

hold us for a while.

Dishes are passed around the table, with the plates before the three diners filling quickly.

Tom: So what have you been doing since last we met, Mr. Twain?

Twain: (waves his hand dismissively) Oh, some more writing. Tried my hand at publishing, but that didn't work out.

Tom: I read *Letters from the Earth*. You let the cynic out.

Twain: Let him out? I suppose. Mostly I was fed up with the way people were so hypocritical. They didn't confront what I said but brushed it aside, suggesting that I was getting old, or that this was my dark period because my wife had died.

Tom: Kill the messenger, ignore the message.

Twain: That's pretty much the way they dealt with new ideas, especially ideas about change. We marginalize the ideator.

Huck: Didn' get no better, neither. Now they wanna kick yer books outta schools, and even burn 'em.

Twain: Because I used what they call the "n-word". That's the way people talked back then, for crying out loud.

Tom: That's the way they talk now, at least in private.

You're right, there are a lot of hypocrites.

Twain: Funny thing is, when I wrote your stories, it was after the Civil War, of course, and things were mean in the South, with the carpetbaggers and all, but a lot of folks down here, they never thought they lost the war, or they didn't lose if fairly or something. They treated their slaves even worse, some of 'em, resenting that they couldn't own 'em anymore.

Huck: But I thought you wrote real opt'mistic-like. That the Injun Joe's 'n dukes 'n kings of this world would get what was comin' to 'em. 'Ventually. I liked that. Gave ya purpose to goin' on when things got tough.

Twain: That's the way I felt, Huck. I wrote your stories more than a decade after the war, at a time when I felt proud of our country. It was pretty impressive that we kept together and got rid of enslaving people.

Tom: Is that why you think we fought the war? Over slavery?

Twain: I think you can point to economic issues, slavery was one of them, that caused the war to start, but I think in the minds of most people today, and probably back then, it was about slavery and how it wasn't really all right. A lot of the people in the south knew inside it was wrong, but the culture prevented them from speaking from their hearts. Too much to go against.

Huck: I'd say most people in the south knew it was wrong...if you count the black folk, too.

Twain and Tom nod affirmatively.

Huck: As I said, I did a lotta travelin' 'round the world. Like a journalist, Mr. Twain, like you, except I hain't been writin' anythin' down. (taps his temple) Got it up here, though. And I was wondering what you think is the American people. I mean, I heard a lot from 'Mericans 's well 's furriners 'bout who we are. As a people, you know. Like the French are French and the English are English, but who are we 'Mericans?

Twain: (looks at Huck pensively for a minute) That's the question, isn't it? We don't really know who we are, as a people, do we?

Tom: I don't know that we have a national character.

Twain: We're very scattered. Think of how different are New Englanders or people from the South, or Midwesterners and Californians.

Tom: Is there an American template that encompasses them all?

They sit it silence for a moment.

Huck: (pensively) I think there is. I don't know if anyone could tell you what it is, we all bein' so dif'ren' as you say, but we know what it means to be an American (taps his chest) inside.

Tom: Huck's right, and it's more than patriotism. It's a feeling about bringing freedom to people around the world, and standing up for the little guy against the bully.

Twain: Is that a realistic view? Sounds like rose-colored glasses.

Tom: Realistic? I think it's what people think is who we are, deep down, if we were really called upon to tap into what it really means to be an American.

Twain: I would like to think so.

Huck: Me, too, but I'm gettin' a little worried that we've been outta practice.

Tom: What do you mean?

Huck: It's been a while since we tapped into that, whatever you call it. Maybe not for fifty years. Before K'rea and V'tnam.

Twain: Huck's right in that sense, about war, but I think the communications revolution that we're pioneering is part of the American spirit, don't you?

Huck: (nods) Sure, yer right, Mr. Twain.

Tom: A fellow I know observed that there had been five revolutions in the United States started in the 1960's. Consumerism, environmentalism, an end to war, an end to racial bias, and an end to gender discrimination. Each one of those could have torn another society apart. But we took on these transformations and less than a half-century later, the right of women and blacks are codified in our laws, consumers have an inherent right to be protected from fraud, and the environment is a global issue.

Twain: We still have our little wars. There are dozens of them around the world, and we've likely as not sold weapons to both sides.

Tom: That's true, and sure none of the five transformations is done being fought, but we turned the corner. America said no to war and discrimination, and yes to consumers and the environment. And we did it all in the space of a few years.

Twain: Not to mark down your enthusiasm, but we didn't pass the equal rights amendment.

Tom: (rueful) I didn't say the struggles were over, but I think we could win if we put our minds and hearts to it. That's who Americans are.

Huck: When I was in France, some'n gave me Mister 'Tocqueville's *Democracy in America*. Ya know, he traveled all 'round the eastern part of the U.S. startin' in the 1831? He wrote we were a country of individu'-lists, which I guess we think is a good thing, but he thought we were takin' it too far. He also said that we might go a little overboard thinkin' on the equality issue. That was while we still have slaves.

Twain: I was young when he was fresh, and I remember feeling a chill when he wrote, "There exists also in the human heart a depraved taste for equality, which impels the weak to attempt to lower the powerful to their own level, and reduces men to prefer equality in slavery to inequality with freedom." I met Alexis many years later; I think he was right.

Huck: Mr. Twain, do you think we're gonna get 'rselves outta this fix? Can we touch that core part of America that's good 'n remember that?

Twain: When I wrote about you boys, I thought it was possible. Now, well I know it's possible, but I don't see how we get there.

Tom: Not without some terribly calamity to pull us together. It always takes a disaster, like Pearl Harbor, and then we start pulling together. Huck, what did you hear when you were abroad? Do people overseas understand us?

Huck: Prob'ly bett'r 'n we do 'rselves, truth be told. But ya know, they're pullin' fer us. They know it's up to us. That 'Merica is the leader, even if we've stumbled some. Funny, I think they might have more confidence in us than we do.

Twain: That's encouraging.

The Waiter approaches the table with plates of a variety of different desserts. As he is placing them on the table, Jim approaches from behind.

Jim: So ah guess mah cookin' ain't so bad. Y'all's still

sittin' upright?

They shower him with a chorus of praise.

Huck: I gotta ask, Jim, when did ya learn 'bout cookin'. We ate good on the raft, but not like this.

They all laugh.

Jim: Mars Huck, I always know'd 'bout cookin' 'n food, since ah wuz a bit 'v a boy, half yer age when we wuz on duh raf'.

Huck: Where'd it go then, 'cause I never saw you over a fire at the Widow's?

Jim: Couldn' show it, Mars Huck, toth'rwise day wud ha' sol' ole Jim for moh money, away from his wife 'n li'l Uns.

Huck gives Jim a hug: It was a different time.

Jim: 'Twas so, Mars Huck.

Tom: Anything you miss about the old days, Jim?

Jim: (his demeanor slips) You, boys. I miss bein' 'round the two of you'se.

Tom: Us? Why?

Jim: Because you be the firs' gen'ration what wasn' gonna have slaves.

Twain: Not because of the war....

Jim: ...Because it was wrong. (pauses) I saw dat in you

boys. I wudda done mos' anything for you to succeed.

Huck: Tom , when you come to Aunt Sally's 'n 'greed to help Jim escape, I thought here you was, Tom Sawyer, helping a black man get free, and that was a surprise. Then when you tol' me he was 'ready free, I'm wonderin' iffn you wudda help'd him 'scape if he warn' free.

Tom: It would have depended on what it was, Huck. I don't discriminate. Though I should say I'm mighty partial to those who save my life.

Jim: (puts his big hands on Tom 's shoulders) Dat's mah honey. (to Twain) You done a mighty-fine job of creatin' these boys, Mr. Twain. You put 'em on a road to bein' fine men.

They look at Twain.

Twain: What's next?

Silence.

Waiter: Coffee?

There were shared nods in favor and he left.

Tom: Oh, I almost forgot. A few years back, I did some *pro bono* work for some environmentalists. They were trying to stop – and we did stop – the building of a Tom Sawyer theme park on Jackson's Island.

Huck and Twain smiled their appreciation but remained silent. Then the young man spoke up.

Huck: Mr. Twain, you seen a lot mor 'n me and Tom.

Twain: I've certainly got some more years on you.

Huck: Well here's what I dunno, and maybe as you do.

Twain nodded his acceptance.

Huck: It's like stopping that merry-go-round on the island. We shoudn 'a had to. It should 'a never been someone's idea.

Twain and Tom showed stunned expressions.

Huck: I mean, ars we e'er gonna do what's right 'cause we're thinkin' right 'stead 'o wrong?

Julia's Closing Remarks

Julia Borden, an attorney, wound up representing herself in a lawsuit against top university officials for their failing to protect her from assaultive behavior by one of their own. From the screenplay, *Truth Be Told*, based on a true story, this is her closing argument to the judge, whose is hearing the case without a jury.

(Julia standing, moves to in front of the plaintiff's table) Thank you, your honor. I grew up with a mother and father who not only had different jobs at work, but they had different jobs in the home. They also had different personalities. But one thing that was always clear to my sister and me was that they were equals. Neither had authority over the other, even though they deferred to each other in certain areas. For instance my mother knew more about what happened in the kitchen and my father more about power tools and keeping engines running, especially in the winter. My mother made sure that her girls had the clothes we needed for school. My father made sure we had plenty of wood for the fire.

I think most families had that kind of division of labor, but I don't know how many taught their children to respect every human being; every human being, without exception or excuse.

I should note that the gender issue was something my father had to learn because he had grown up in a male-dominated society...but my mother was patient with him.

So for their daughters, we always knew our rights, but we weren't so naive as to think that everyone else was aware of them, or believed in them. Especially men but plenty of women too.

My mamma always insisted to us that it wasn't up to any court to give us our rights or to recognize us. She said that no self-respecting woman would spend time with a man who needed the law to tell him how to treat her.

But there are men for whom the law is a barrier, and that barrier must be enforced in a society that considers itself civilized.

There is no defense for the kind of behavior I suffered – for any behavior that demeans, disrespects another human being – and this crime – this shame – is grossly magnified when those in a position to stop it... fail the victim by denying her protection, fail the perpetrator by not forcing him to get help, and fail the society by not assuring justice.

If the defendants truly believe they are innocent of these charges, I truly believe them to be in an ever-shrinking minority.

Here's the real answer to Miz Priestley's title question "So What?" Even with the minimum amount of publicity this case has gotten in the mainstream press, what little coverage there was has apparently resonated quickly and considerably.

We were receiving so many phone calls and emails that we had to get an unlisted number and set up new email accounts. There has been so large a response – since the *Law Times* article on the Internet – that just in the past six months, there have been more than 220,000 contacts. We had to hire a trained screening service to handle all of the calls and the emails, directing many of the correspondents to counseling and legal aid centers when appropriate, and some to law enforcement when there was a sense of urgency.

Your honor, as difficult as the circumstances of this case have been for me personally, and for my family and friends, I am truly optimistic that society is changing. It will take men teaching men and women teaching each other what my parents told us; that all human beings deserve respect just for being human.

I think we went through some confusing times with the so-called women's liberation movement, when we tried to make men and women the same, rather than equal in rights. Because yes, there are essential differences between the genders. Otherwise the species would have died out long ago.

A friend of mine sent me an essay last week that I thought was very telling of our situation in this case. I will read a short part of it.

"On occasion she would dress up, not to the nines, but just in the clothes she liked that she thought she looked good in. And then she would go down to the Oak Room at the Plaza Hotel and sit on one of the high chairs by the bar. She'd be there for a couple of hours, slowly nursing a glass of wine or two. Her intention was not to attract a date, someone to go home with, but just to be found attractive."

Reading that piece reminded me of my early childhood when my daddy would occasionally take me fishing. Every time we went fishing, my daddy would repeat one of his favorite quotes by Henry David Thoreau, who said, "Some men go fishing all of their lives and they don't know it isn't fish they're after."

I wasn't interested in those slimy fish, but I loved the time that I would spend with my daddy, standing in a pool in a river, casting out my line. And waiting for a fish to bite. Truth be told, I didn't much care if they did bite.

We mostly used flies that my daddy had tied himself. He didn't give me the best ones because I had a habit of catching a snag and losing the fly. Around noon, we'd have our sandwiches my mamma had made us; he had a beer and I had my milk. Then I might just sit on the bank, and my daddy would tie on one of his favorite flies and drop it in a pool where he knew the big ones were. He'd almost never get a bite, though he occasionally got a nudge. He was quite content with that. He said he knew the big old fish saw his flies, saw how good he had tied them, and they weren't going to take them from him. That was fine with my father.

So it reminds me of the woman in the bar. She wasn't trying to catch anything. She just wanted respect. No human being is entitled to less.

Nature Is Not the Enemy

There's a degree of irony in President Trump's decla-ration of war on the coronavirus. It's really a war on Nature. Yes, Nature created the virus as part of a three-pronged global renewal program. This is good news over the long term, but not for a great many of the current denizens of the Earth.

Rachel Carson's *Silent Spring*, published in 1962, awakened many of the cognoscenti to the need to protect the environment. But the audience for such concerns grew dramatically when Senator Gaylord Nelson, a Democrat from Wisconsin, observing that most people were not paying attention to the health of the environment, established the first Earth Day on April 22, 1970. Over 20 million people around the world attended festivities that day, and the date has been marked every year since.

That was 50 years ago, and the Earth's population was approaching four billion, which was about twice the carrying capacity of our dear blue planet. So we were already consuming more than we could safely produce, and we were producing more than we could safely dispose of. And it has only gotten worse, much worse.

We are today approaching eight billion people, running out of potable water, out-fishing the oceans, using antibiotics to grow animals faster to slaughter, poisoning the air, polluting our rivers and lakes, and using artificial nutrients to grow our food. The Great Pacific Garbage Patch is now three times the size of France, and there are four other ocean garbage patches around the world. We have not been good stewards of the Earth.

Why? In fairness, some noted efforts were made with the Clean Air and Clean Water Acts (under Richard Nixon, no less), but true progress was held back by the lack of public education to the underlying issues, and an addiction to single-use aluminum and plastic packaging. More crippling was the fact that corporate bottom lines have been the dominant focus of leaders around the world, and looking-the-other-way ignorance has made that possible. Not only has our own government sanctioned the production of pollution from the plastics, chemicals, fossil fuels, agriculture, metals, technologies, and other major industries, but the citizens have, through their consumption and other behavioral patterns, endorsed the pollution policies. Americans throw away 60 million plastic water bottles every day.

Beyond the hard evidence in our polluted land, water,

and air there is an attitude by the primary offenders that reeks of arrogant dismissal. At the 25th U.N. Climate Change Conference in Madrid last December representatives of the fossil fuel industry effectively refused to acknowledge their responsibility or to do anything reduce their output. Shortly after the conference, Trump tweeted a slap at climate crisis activist Greta Thunberg that "Greta must work on her Anger Management problem," and later tweeted at the 16-year-old, "Chill Greta, Chill!"

So what has changed? Nature is intervening. She has watched us move past the tipping point in population and pollution and is now moving to reverse course and restore the environment. She will upend our lifestyles because the way we have been living is antithetical to preserving the natural environmental balance on the Earth. She has taken action to accomplish this – it has to be said – noble task although it will be historically difficult and painful over a number of generations.

First was global warming, which was renamed *climate change* to soften the sound of the problem so more people would voice their concerns about it. But it was still about temperatures rising because of pollution in the atmosphere, mostly from the processing and use of fossil fuels. Both poles began melting, as did the Greenland ice sheet, which is increasingly in danger of sliding into the North Atlantic. That would raise the seas worldwide by a conservative estimate of several feet. Over 40% of Americans, and many people around the world, live in coastal regions.

Also melting is the now-misnamed permafrost, and that means the release of massive amounts of methane gas which will quicken the pace of the warming. If you've been paying attention, you also know that virtually every new report on climate change raises two alarms. One is that the change is greater than scientists previously had measured, and two is that it's happening faster than before.

Climate change doesn't just affect the melting ice sheets and glaciers. Warmer temperatures mean less snow accumulation which, in many areas, means less water saved for summer and fall It changes the weather. Not only are weather systems moving out of traditional patterns, but they are often carrying more moisture, causing historic floods. Hurricanes are stronger and more frequent, as are tornados. This means not only more damage of personal property and injuries and deaths, but reduction of arable land, the collapse of bridges and highways, power outages, and the ripping apart of tanks holding toxic waste. And we are seeing stronger dry winds knocking down power poles and fanning deadly fires.

It won't be long before the weather is doing more damage to distribution and communications systems than we can keep up with. Those daily deliveries of primary needs – food, medicine, and other basic supplies – will be jeopardized. Considering the hoarding of toilet paper we saw with the early scare about the coronavirus, it is easy to image the panic that will set in over the store shelves being cleared of all food-stuffs. No wonder the sale of guns and ammunition has, pardon the expression, shot through the roof.

Speaking of the coronavirus...Too many people are without the facts, which is understandable since no one knows where this global disaster is headed. The numbers are already bad, and the failure of govern-ments to have prepared for a pandemic will likely take a high toll. Some people insist that the virus is a deliberate plot by the Chinese to undermine the U.S. especially, and others are convinced that it is the work of the New World Order. The truth is that this pan-demic is the second prong Mother Nature's plan to restore balance to the global environment. But while Covid-19 will likely reduce the world population by tens – maybe hundreds – of millions, that is nowhere near the reduction needed to get our environment in balance.

The real effect of the virus is what it is doing to the world's economies. Tens of trillions of dollars are being wiped off the books, and billions of people will be driven into poverty, and starvation. This will cripple most, if not all, governments, at least to some degree. Combined with the effects of the more violent and destructive weather, a great many nations will be fractured as people are forced back into reorganization as self-sustaining communities. While we can presume that there will be a sea change in our use of resources and our production of waste, the ramifications of this transition from our current lifestyle are all but beyond imagination.

So what about that over-population problem? The climate change and the coronavirus – and whatever additional plagues will be born – aren't going to reduce the ten-figure population, not by themselves. There is a third arrow Mother Nature has in her quiver. A clue about it is suggested by the frequency that one hears people use the expression, "That's crazy." It might be meant as a euphemism but what they are truly describing is insanity. Professionals and academics might use complex terms to describe the various behaviors, but all fall under the simple definition of extreme foolishness or irrationality.

A key indicator of insanity is suicide, both attempted and completed. The numbers have been rising significantly in the United States over the last twenty years. Not counted in those rising numbers are the tens of thousands of opioid overdoses. Also not factored into this picture are the 40+% of Americans who are obese, the 30+% who are serious alcoholics, the 34 million who smoke cigarettes, and the 15% rise in people suffering "accidental" deaths.

There is also plenty of insanity that is not fatally self-destructive. For instance, almost half of the more than a half-million homeless people in our country are mentally ill. There are people with various addictions that reduce their safety and security, such as gambling and street racing. But perhaps the most terrifying of the insane are those who don't choose right over wrong. Yes, there are those making money poisoning the planet. But consider also the physically violent who beat their spouses and children. And those who take the further step of killing or maiming other people out of anger, or greed.

(Isn't it curious that when someone commits a particularly heinous murder, a jury is asked to question the killer's sanity, to mediate whether he goes to prison or an insane asylum? As though someone who commits a murder out of anger or greed isn't deemed to be insane; that it's somehow sane to kill another human being for money or spite?)

There are lesser degrees of insanity, of course. For instance, living in a modern society that is rife with racism and extremist behavior at both ends of the political spectrum, from the resurgent Nazis to the far lefties up in arms over cultural appropriation. David Hawkins produced a scale of consciousness that weighed such important human qualities as self-awareness, compassion, and integrity, and he found that 85% of the people on the planet are of negative consciousness, being controlled by such characteristics as guilt, grief, apathy, anger, shame, and fear. It's an understandable assessment considering the scope of poverty, oppression, and violence in our world today; conditions that would be mitigated if we weren't so over-populated.

This final point about how insanity plays in Nature's program. In a poem written by Longfellow in 1875, was the, "Whom the gods would destroy they first make mad." There's considerable history to that. As Rebecca Costa noted in her important bestseller, *The Watchman's Rattle*, major civilizations rose on intelligence and responsible leadership, and then collapsed from inattentiveness in the arms of religion.

And here we are today with politicians and judges giving ever more authority to churches while taking away long-valued human rights. They also bend to Big Pharma, Wall Street, the gun lobby, the farmers poisoning the bees on which we count for our food, the airlines which cram us into ever smaller spaces, and social media channels which have given voice to the most corrupt and depraved villains in society. That's crazy.

What good does it do to know of Nature's program? Is this just a depressing doomsday prognostication? No, to the second question. The answer to the first question is that we should know what we're dealing with, because only then can we change our thinking and work toward possible solutions. But first we have to check our negative attitude at the door. Nature isn't doing this to punish us.

We too easily anthropomorphize what we face in life, for instance referring to unexplainable events as *acts of*

God, and that breeds confusion and misdirection for people seeking true explanations. It's like thinking of a great white shark as being evil. It's not malicious in attacking the swimmer; it's going for lunch, to survive. Similarly with Nature. Nature isn't angry with us. (I'd like to think she's disappointed but not angry.) She just needs to fix what we have broken by failing to limit the population to the Earth's carrying capacity, and by allowing the miscreants in our global society to put personal enrichment ahead of the sanctity of the planet's environment.

So how to do we find out what we need to do so as to obviate the full package of Nature's plan? Understand that if we don't, we will wind up where we are now headed. We have to put on our thinking caps and come up with sound answers to four questions. (1) Where are we now? A no-holds-barred description of the mess we're in. (2) How did we get here? This is not about blame but to identify our wrong decisions; though it is useful to recognize who got us into this mess so we can devalue any further contributions they might offer. (3) Where do we want to go? We need to define in practical terms what are realistic goals, both for the relatively short term and for down the road. And (4) How do we get there? We need to map out the logical steps that must be taken, according to a reasonable schedule, with the recognition that there will be tweaks and maybe wholesale changes along the way.

Remember what Einstein said when we exploded the

first atomic bombs in 1945. "The release of atomic power has changed everything except our way of thinking." And he added that "the solution to this problem lies in the heart of mankind." There may have never been a greater truth.

Some other truths we have to accept and invoke that most of what we spend on things military needs to be shifted to new science for non-polluting energy production – think solar – transportation systems, recyclable distribution, food production, and domestic security. We need to reformat out educational programs so they engage children with noble values, healthy purpose, and a sense of responsibility; providing them with the information they will need in growing more advanced ideas for a better future. And we need to support only those peoples that live in peace and reduce their populations by not having so many children; viz, Paul Ehrlich's 1968 bestseller *The Population Bomb*.

While much needs to be done to reverse the current course, it is a viable alternative to the woeful wringing of hands. This coronavirus has given us a wake-up call. We won't be able to go back to the way we were. Like the all too familiar response to someone complaining about the aches and pains and other anomalies of getting old, it's better than the alternative.

Bienvenue Vingt-Quatorze

(*Welcome 2014*)

We are very glad, I think, to be through 2013, that for so many has been a very difficult year. For some, the financial side has been severely challenging. But I'm thinking more of angst we have all felt watching what has happened to our country. The failure to restore millions of our fellow Americans to economic security after The Great Recession; the refusal to give food stamps to feed the 16 million American children who don't get enough to eat; and our tragic descent into a society where faux security fears erode our cherished right to privacy. Not to mention the continuing subsidizing of fossil fuels while our global climate degrades into a fury of ever-strengthening storms.

But 2014 may well see a turn-around. There is a New Moon, which is an unusual co-incident event for the beginning of the New Year, and it may well auger important change. I think in this remarkably tumultuous and uncertain time that transformation – on various levels – will be charging through both our personal and outside lives.

Maybe we are entering an era of taking ourselves more seriously, of reaching beyond our rights to our responsibilities. It will be a time for us to take back the reins of our lives and remake ourselves and our communities, both local and global.

The philosopher Abraham Maslow would ask high school-age students, "Who among you is going to be great?" And when, predictably, no one raised their hands, he asked, "Who else then?"

Indeed, that is the question today more than ever, and the answer is <u>we</u> are going to be great and <u>we</u> are going to show our great-ness to a greatness-hungry world. For if not we, well...that's how we got to where we are today, finding ourselves in such need.

In writing this, there was, curiously, a line in my head from the Gettysburg address. Speaking of the work to be done, Lincoln said, "It is for us the living...." And it is ever more so for us today, when much is in crisis, and we can no longer kick the proverbial can down the street.

We must see our lives in a new light, and accept our roles as the shapers of a better world. Our lives must be about honoring those leaders who have come before us and hallowing the ground for the generations to follow us.

We can do this in ways that may seem small but that can make a difference.

We must look upon those who cross our paths as fellow human beings; as delicate and as strong and as noble as are we. And we can hold in our hearts the belief that they, too, are ready to raise themselves up to meet their potential.

We can live in grace with a longer smile, we can look in people's eyes to show our commitment, we can show our love when we give, and when we receive.

So under the New Moon, atop the New Year, let us resolve to make this a better world. For as Tina Turner sang, "We don't need another hero." In truth, we must be the heroes of our own time.

* * * * *

UPDATE: June 2020 - Our situation has gotten significantly more serious over the past six years. This past year alone has all too well served my prognostication first delivered last spring: *Anything can happen... and it will.*

Ukraine, impeachment, coronavirus, the upending of the global economy, the effect of the death of George Floyd, and demonstrations worldwide for demanding an end to racism and injustice. Plus there's climate change and a social schism ranging from resurgent fascism on the right to eat-their-young social extremism on the left. The words to describe what is happening and what might be our future seem quite inadequate to embrace the possibilities.

We each have some to contribute, and we should consider what that might be so when the time comes to add our chips to the pot, it won't come as a surprise that might upset the applecart. Understand that success will not be produced from hope and wishful thinking, but from the mind and heart, character and purpose. And as Maslow put it, "If not you, then who will answer the call."

Say It Write

About the Author

Tony Seton is a journalist, writer, publisher, public speaker, business/political consultant, and communications specialist. As an award-winning broadcast journalist for ABC TV, he covered Watergate, six elections, and five space shots. And he produced Barbara Walters' news interviews, and business/economics coverage.

Later, he wrote and produced two award-winning public television documentaries. He has conducted over 2,600 interviews, and is the author of more than 2,300 essays.

Through Seton Publishing, Tony has edited and published more than 40 of his own books and screenplays, and 30+ for clients.

As a political consultant, his clients have included Nancy Pelosi, Tom Campbell, the American Nurses Association, and a plethora of local candidates.

He has taught journalism and writing, provided media training, and produced websites.

Tony is also a private pilot and a photographer.

SETON
PUBLISHING